SIGN UP FOR UPDATES

For updates about new releases, sign up for the mailing list below. You'll know as soon as I release new books, including my upcoming new series, titled *King's Gate,* as well as sequels in the *Future Reborn* series.

https://www.subscribepage.com/y3s8n6

FUTURE RESHAPED

BOOK 3 IN THE FUTURE REBORN SERIES

DANIEL PIERCE

CONTENTS

1

THE WATER POURED past me in silence, a bloom of dirt turning the channel from clear to brown. Something was in the sluice ahead, and it wasn't human.

I pointed to the water, earning a grim nod from Mira, who unshouldered her rifle without a sound. I did the same with my shotgun, then began to move forward in a low crouch. Overhead, the sun was brilliant, though the air still held the chill of a winter night. It might have been February in the old world, but things like that didn't matter as much now. We had other concerns, like why one of our scouts had gone missing. We were at the farthest edge of a new expansion on the eastern side of The Free Oasis; a place of few trees and long channels that carried the new water source away in radial canals. The water would be the lifeblood of our second section; a place that could hold another 2000 people or more once it was fully forested and settled.

The rules were simple. We planted as we went, and we built in between the trees. I was determined to reclaim the desert from whatever calamity created it when the virus split humanity into a broken tumble of beings, all struggling to survive among the monsters. Some humans had *become* monsters, like the ogres and their kin. We didn't even know just how far humans had diverged, and without communication over long distances, the only way to know was to see for ourselves.

There was little cover ahead, which meant the creature—be it good or bad—was in the channel. It still didn't explain the missing scout, or even why there was no sign of life around us. Even in the raw expanse of The Empty, that was off.

Mira pointed to the channel ahead of us, and I froze. Bobbing in the water was the remains of boot, the sole torn away, the top punctured in a row of marks that could have only been made by large, sharp teeth. "It's there."

"Whe--oh. Shit." I shook my head in disgust.

"Lizards." One word, but many meanings, and no end to the variation. This one was a mottled brown, its face smeared with gore as it worried at what looked suspiciously like a human ribcage.

"Too many lizards," Mira agreed. She aimed her rifle, but I shook my head, holstering the shotgun as I slid my blades free. The lizard was three meters of killer, but that was no reason to waste ammunition. Plus, under the mud and gore, the hide looked interesting; a pebbled affair with swirls of color that would yield a lot of leather, given a little work.

I made my decision.

Stalking forward, I got to within arm's length of the beast as it cracked into a femur, the gunshot sound of breaking bone almost enough to make me twitch. *The neck. It had to be the neck.* I jumped, both blades coming inward as hard as my muscles could drive them, the steel sinking into the creature's musclebound neck and punching out through the other side to graze my forearms.

I hadn't quite thought that part through.

The creature shuddered and died, the human femur still in its wide, lethal jaws.

"Stabbed yourself, Canan?" Mira asked, walking forward with a lazy smile. She liked taunting me with stories from my own time, even if she butchered the names.

"It's Conan, and no. I grazed myself, which is a huge difference. Heroes suffer grazing wounds, only idiots stab themselves," I told her while grimacing at the stinging cuts on both arms.

"Right," she said with a smirk. She put her boot on the creature's head. It looked tiny against the long, cavernous skull. "Who's in his mouth? Or her mouth? I can never tell with lizards."

"Might be a he. We'll know after we rinse the hide. As to the poor bastard he's eating, I have no idea if it isn't the scout. We're not missing anyone else that I can think of, are we?" I asked.

"No. Head count was solid this morning. Two hundred sixteen and growing, all with their heads." Mira looked at the remains, then shrugged. "That was a man. Scrawny, if his leg is any sign."

"So not one of ours. A wanderer?" I asked, staring into The Empty. There was no sign of a cart, or wagon. No fires and no campsite. Whoever the man had been, he was dead and most likely forgotten, just another victim of a world that truly had no fucks to give. There were shreds of clothing, but nothing that could be considered a uniform or closely paired with a certain occupation, like a trader or smith. I shrugged, trying and failing to hide an attitude of callousness. Sometimes, the best thing to do for the dead was move on. They would never know.

I thumped a boot into the lizard's back. "I'll start at the belly. Help me flip him over?"

We rolled the creature over, exposing a cream-colored stomach with smaller scales. There were scars on the stomach; a record of a life filled with fighting. I slipped a blade home and began to cut, humming to myself as the lizard went from predator to resource with the slice of steel.

We were all just a cut away from being in the same place out here in The Empty, which meant the only thing that mattered was to make sure you were the one holding the blade.

2

"MAKE THAT TWO HUNDRED AND"—SILK looked over my shoulder, her full lips moving silently —"twenty-one. A family came in from the north while you were out."

"Any critical skills?" I asked, tossing the rolled lizard hide to the ground. It hit with a wet thump, and I nodded at two kids who were approaching. "Take that to the tannery, if you would. I'll be along with instructions." The boys pelted away, hide swinging between them as they laughed at the reeking mass. I'd see to it that they got one of the small pies we were baking at the community oven.

"The grandmother, Beba, is a capable doctor. One of the grandkids nearly lost an ear to a raptor.

Her stitches were damn fine work," Silk said approvingly. "The dad is built like a bull, kids are good, and the wife has experience with papermaking."

"Papermaking? I didn't even know people did that," I said.

"If there are materials. I'm more interested in finding out if she can make fabric. Paper and torn linen are close cousins. Might be that she can open a store of her own."

"See that she gets a stall in the market, and let them pick their job. The dad's big, you say?" I asked.

"Huge. A hand taller than you and half again your weight. Carries a—well, I guess it's a club with a spike on the end, on his back. He's a friendly sort, too. They brought two wagons and some Hightec. They made their way along the remains of that highway that the storm exposed," Silk said, waving a fine-boned hand at her neck while she held her black curls up. Her green eyes were narrowed in thought, and she was radiant, as usual.

I was washing myself in the sink. We had water run to more homes each day, especially since two of our newcomers were natural born plumbers. They'd taken to calling themselves the Waterboys, and with enough salvage and creativity, we were going to have a decent water infrastructure. "What's the big guy's name?"

"Breslin. His wife is"—Silk looked at her notebook—"Jossi. He had some tools with him when they were choosing a building site. Said something about sandstone and—well, I wasn't listening. I was admiring Beba's library. She has books and things."

"Sandstone? Huh. Only one way to find out what he does. Point me to them."

Silk took my hand and we began walking. The Oasis was growing at a rate limited only by how fast trees could be planted. As it turned out, water, sun, and importing fertilizer made for a long growing season in The Empty. The central canopy was pushing outward with each month, and houses were built on regular lines, following the radial water channels as they ran toward the desert.

"Three years, in case you're wondering," she said.

"Then what?" I asked her, looking down. Her role in The Oasis added to her beauty, if anything. Her black curls were pulled away from a face dominated by luminous green eyes. When she smiled, it was a different thing than the night we first met. Her smile was joyous rather than calculating. It looked good on her.

She pointed to an invisible place beyond us. "The trees will be stable in four different hubs. We'll have water, housing, and services for each zone. You can let them send representatives to the council."

"What council?"

"The one you're going to form. I know how you think. You're not a warlord, Jack, despite your own fears. I spoke to Andi. She told me of your Caesar and Stalin and President Ruston. You're nothing like them, Jack. You don't want what they had, and you won't allow anyone else to take it. It's only logical to think that the next step is government by the people, as long as they don't open us up to risk." She stopped, taking both of my hands. "We can't descend into—into what there was before. At The Outpost. I won't go back to that."

"I would never let it happen. Nor would you, or Mira, and certainly not Andi. She's fresh off the exact thing that killed eight billion people," I said.

"As long as we understand our goals are one

and the same, I'm yours." She stood on her tiptoes to kiss me.

I met her halfway. "They are."

"Good. Now let's go see this big bastard and find out what he can do with that club."

3

"I'M BRESLIN, and my family is . . . scattered for the moment, it seems." He shook my hand with care. I have big hands. He had paws, not hands, with fingers thickened by callouses.

"You've got the hands of someone who knows their way around work. Got a specialty?" I asked him, smiling. He was big, but there was no air of violence around him. He had the look of a father who happened to be built like a tank. He had brown eyes and black hair, his skin darkened to the color of tea by sunshine, and a lot of it. He made his living outside, if I was guessing.

"Stonework. I was in the guild at Kassos, but —" He paused and spat on the ground, the first hint of aggression I'd seen from him in our brief meeting. "Thieves and liars were the best of what the guild had to offer. When we could, we left. For here."

"Here?" I asked him, my brow going up in surprise.

"The Oasis. You're Jack, right? We know about you. Know about how you gave Wetterick a lesson, and we know of your place. It sounded a far cry better than that stinking sewer," he said.

"Kassos is that bad?" Silk asked.

"And more. Are you the—is this your place too?" Breslin asked Silk, his face uncertain.

"Silk, formerly Lady Silk of The Outpost, and yes, this is also my place. I'm with Jack, and we're glad you've come. Point me to your family so I can help them settle?"

If Breslin knew what Silk had been, he made no show if it. "They were going to the center, to find out about supplies."

"Then I know where they are. Welcome, Breslin." Silk moved away with the grace of a breeze, and Breslin stood watching her for a moment, then closed his jaw. "I—sorry. Meant no offense. She's a rare one."

"None taken, and she is. The four of us—"

"Four of you? You mean there are more women in your, ah—home?" Breslin asked.

"Yes. You'll meet them soon enough." We stood in awkward silence while he processed that information, then he smiled.

"You seemed excited to find out I do stone work. What does the Free Oasis need of me?" he asked.

I examined the growing sprawl of our home. "In a word, everything."

Breslin exhaled, then jerked a huge thumb back toward an old but well-kept wagon. "I have tools. What do you need first?"

"Your home," I replied.

"Home?" he asked, brow lowered in confusion.

"Build your home first. With our help, of course, and then we can discuss a list. Our greatest needs are foundations for houses and means to keep water in small channels, and then come the roads. We have ample stone but no real experience doing it, unless you count our records Andi and Silk are poring over. We're not just going to build a camp here, Breslin. Do you understand what I mean by that?"

"You want . . . a city?" he asked.

"For starters. We're going to give people a safe

place, away from that shithole Kassos and every other amateur dictator who's carved this land up. We have Hightec, and a lot of it. I'd be lying if I said your arms weren't going to prove useful, but your mind is just as valuable to me. To us," I said.

"If you're building all that, then I have a third quality you'll want to use, and the good news is it will cost you nothing."

"Which is?" I asked.

"I will fight. You know others will come, and not all of them intend on being a part of something. They'll want what you have. I heard nothing of your Hightec, but someone has, and they'll come for it. For you, and Silk, and all of this," he said, his tone colored with regret.

"I know. We expect it, and sooner rather than later." I clapped him on an enormous shoulder and pointed to the horizon. "We have a network building, and with it, I'm going to reestablish a place where children can grow up. Where people will get old, instead of dead at thirty. Or sooner. Trust me, whoever chooses to invade us makes a fatal mistake. I'll see to that."

He nodded, then turned his grin to me. "In that case, we have a lot of work to do. Show me this water you need shaped. I have a few ideas."

"See the channels that run from our main springs?" I asked.

"Radial, small, protected. All good things to carry the water farther. I assume you want to expand the system?" Breslin turned in place, his eyes taking in every detail.

"We have three more springs located. What would you do to replicate this system, or even improve on it?"

He pulled at his chin, then gestured that I should lead. "Show me one of the sites? I'd rather know what I'm working with before making promises."

"I like that. This way," I said, striding off to the closest water source we'd found. It was to the east, where the succulents gave away a hidden cache of water. It was also close to Derin and Scoot's forge, which they brought with them from The Outpost. Derin and his daughter were invaluable for his skill and her role as his assistant. Their craft—metal-working--- would need a considerable portion of the water in order to assure their productivity.

In minutes, we were standing in the bright sun, staring down a clear pool surrounded by green, living things on three sides.

"Does it overflow? Ah, okay. I see." Breslin knelt

by the small trickle that led away. The stream was knee deep, but the flow was good and, more concerning, underused. He rubbed his head, thinking, then stood with an air of decision. "Tell me more about your plan for this part of the settlement. Will you use the same model? Channels, trees, and homes?"

"Right. Same thing, but Derin and Scoot—that's their place over there—will be here, along with space for a few more craft people. Leather, fabric. Maybe some printing. It won't be purely industrial, but more of a mixed area," I said.

"Then the first thing I would do is stone the walls, build up a reservoir, and decide where the homes will be. I like this setting, but the water will only flow so far if trees are using it. I don't know anything about trees, so we'll need someone to take a guess," he said.

"Let's say a hundred meters, maximum, for each channel. We can fit twenty buildings around this, along with open space and enough tree cover to protect the gardens. If we have to, we can dig this spring out, or see if we can punch through the water table nearby. We have access to data that might let us do just that," I said. I didn't mention what Andi had at her fingertips because I didn't know Breslin well enough to reveal our second and third sites.

"That makes sense. So I'll need access to sandstone or something harder, and I can build the channels first, then cut out the connections and let the water run. Might be a good idea to have a small pond at the end of one of the channels, just in case we get a heavy rain. And you know we will. I've seen evidence of the storms that blow through here. It's better to have a place for all that water to go," Breslin said.

"There's a ridge just west of us that's nothing but rock. I can take you there later, and we can stake the channels. You'll have help, by the way. New arrivals work on their own homes. The sweat makes them care for it more. Like an investment," I said.

"Good plan." He scanned the distance, then looked back at me, his eyes questioning. "What about defense?"

"For now, we have active defenses that you can't see, but trust me when I say it's unlike anything you've known. Later, we'll build walls, if only to contain our growth as it happens. We're here for the long haul, and that means building smart, not just throwing places up for the purpose of a roof," I said.

"We saw monsters in the desert. Things I never imagined, or at least signs of them. Tracks, scat. Bones. I'm not going to lie, a wall would make me feel a lot better, especially knowing my children only have a wagon to protect them," he said.

"What about two walls? Or even three?" I asked.

"Go on."

I knelt and began scratching a rough diagram in the dirt. "I see us growing in a pattern, sure, but there's more to it than that. We're going to establish The Oasis as a hub for control, law, and commerce. But that's the beginning, because I know there's a shitstorm on the horizon. There always is," I said.

"And you're going to make concentric rings of control, to fall back in case a large force of—people? Creatures? What?" Breslin asked.

"People worry me more than monsters. I can handle most animals by myself, and they actually serve a purpose for us."

"Meat? Hide?" he asked. "What else?"

"They're a threat. Not the kind of vague bullshit people use to control the masses. They're a real, tangible threat to show people that just because we're building a stable city, the land around us is vicious. It will *always* find a way to kill you, because this world is not civilized. Not even a little bit. The virus left life in such disarray, I wouldn't be surprised if a dragon came flying overhead. I don't want to lose people, and I want us to be safe, but—"

"A good jolt of reality wouldn't hurt now and then, eh? Especially if it has claws. Or wings. Or Both," Breslin said, laughing easily.

"Exactly. And that's just one of the big-ticket items I have in mind, along with a thousand others. We'll never recreate the urban decay of— ah, where I'm from, which means we have to start with a better foundation, and lay plans for a fight against nature that will never end," I said.

Breslin gave me a measured look, and when he spoke, it was in a slow, deliberate tone. "I know you might want to reveal all your plans to me. I'm an outsider. But your desire to hide where you're from doesn't really matter to me, Jack. I don't care, and it's a little late to close your jaw now, don't you think?"

I smiled at him. He was quick, and more importantly, he was right. "I guess if you're in on our future defenses, the possibility you're a spy for an invading army is irrelevant. You could just build a door and let them walk right in," I said.

"And poison your water, or some other cowardly act," he said.

"Cowardice is another word for sneaky, especially when you're fighting giant lizards. Or ogre things with human flesh stuck in their teeth," I said.

"It was you. I'll be damned. Hardhead?" Hardhead *had* been a monstrous, cannibalistic creature with a bounty on his head. I took his head, and then I took the bounty.

"My work, yes. I'd just arrived in town, so to speak. Had to earn a little coin before I knew what my next step was going to be," I admitted.

"I went the same route, but without the heroics."

"There was nothing heroic about how Hardhead smelled," I said, earning a bark of laughter from Breslin.

"Still, I came into the city from a settlement to the north. Low hills where my family was able to scrape by as ranchers. A hard life, but I took to the hammer at a young age. I was always finding bones and such, but from old creatures long past," Breslin said.

"Fossils? That's what got you working stone?"

"Among other things. Being this size helped," he said, and it was my turn to laugh.

"Sometimes, we're built for a certain job. Need anything from me right now?" I asked him.

"I'll unload the wagons and then wrangle the kids later. Is there a community meal tonight?"

"Sunset. In the center, and I'll show you the facility under us. It's part greenhouse, power center, and storage, but that's all changing since we found Andi. She's both engineer and advisor, and we can all talk tonight. We've got a surprise for everyone. The good kind." I peered up at the sun. It would be a full afternoon of work, and by the time the fire was going, I would be ready for some quiet. "Meet me at the fire, and we'll go from there."

"Until then," Breslin said, clasping my hand and moving off. He was grinning like a man who's just found the kind of job security one can only dream of, and he was right.

4

EVERYONE MILLED around nibbling at roasted bird while we waited for the main course, an enormous rattler that would easily feed an army. Three people took turns basting the creature, which was curled up and stuck with metal rods to hold it in place over the glowing coals. As barbecue went, it was quite different than anything from my time, but for now, it smelled incredible.

Mira poked the snake with a knife, nodded, and pronounced it done. "Grab a plate and come on. Veggies are here, herbs are chopped, and we've got some flatbread for the drippings. There's plenty. Don't be shy."

People began moving into a line, parents pushing their kids ahead, with several of the men holding back. Breslin and Derin were in conversation, smiling and chatting in what could only be good for The Oasis. I waited too as the line thinned. There was plenty of rattler to go around, and by the time I made my way to the food, people were settled on the ground, talking and eating in a companionable hum.

"Snake?" Breslin asked.

"Better than almost anything except those big hogs. We eat birds, and even the occasional unidentified critter. Fish, too, when we can get it, but the rattlers are—well, I won't say *easy* to kill, but there are plenty of them around," I said, peeling the snakeskin back from the white flesh and slicing some away with my knife. We had plates and cups and cutlery; all courtesy of the stores underneath and what our new arrivals brought with them. As a community, we were reaching a point where people could stock their homes and not give everything away. It was a good sign, and we were about to have an even better one as the sun set.

Andi slid next to me, a grin on her lips, her hazel eyes twinkling with excitement. Her blonde hair had gotten longer, but she still looked like an elven maiden to me. Her smile deepened as I admired her. "Ready," she said.

"Do the honors? It's your baby," I said.

"Happy to. Mira helped, along with a few others. With a crew of six, we can complete beyond the borders of the forest, right out into The Empty, if that's what you want," Andi said.

"I think that sounds like a huge step forward," I said.

"Was hoping you'd say that. It's time to reclaim this world. We start here, and that's not the only good news."

"I'm listening," I said, leaning close enough to smell the spice of her skin. She was glowing with excitement and it made her even more beautiful.

"I finished prepping the solar trucks. They'll carry a ton at minimum, and roll over anything in this godforsaken desert. They've got a range of eighty klicks a day and you can start using them right away. Parked at our place, under the trees."

"That's a game changer. Any chance there are more stashed away?" I asked her.

She kissed my forehead, chuckling. "I'm sure of it, but I need to dive into the manifests that were updated after I went in the tube. Silk can help while you and Mira bring home the bacon."

"Thanks, babe." I looked around at the people and nodded to her. "Your show."

Andi stood and clapped her hands. "Listen up. A lot of work went into this next trick, and there's more where that came from." She walked to a post and I heard a distinct click.

Lights flared into life along the center pathway, drawing a gasp and then applause.

"I'll be damned," Breslin said. "Power. Real, steady power."

"And more where that came from. We had a source underneath us, in the facility, but that's no longer necessary. I'll be upfront with you. We have a reactor, and we can light up the entire area if we want. We're going to run lights, but each home will have power, too. We're done with camping out. From here on, we don't just survive. We solidify our hold on this place and push outward. No matter what," I told him.

"Why do I feel like that was a question?" Breslin asked me.

"Because it was. You're either in or out, and I need that hammer you brought swinging as soon as possible. What do you think?"

He smiled and unfolded a scrap of paper. "I made a few notes this afternoon, ranking the projects that I can do by importance to everyone here. Before I say anything, I'm going to need a team. I can't do waterworks by myself, and I think you're going to like my other ideas even more."

"You've got it. How many?"

"Twenty to start," he said without flinching. "Not water channels."

"The roads, then? That's your first item?" I asked.

"How did you guess?" He laughed, then began to read the other items. "Three days to lay the base for my house. My family can work on it, and I can do split time between the road and home. I'm guessing that reactor didn't come from the facility under our feet?"

"You would be right," I said in a neutral tone.

"Then you'll want to connect us to wherever the other settlement is. And that means stabilizing a road that is, at best, a ruin. There's only one way to do that. I think," he said.

"Tell me."

"We take what's left of the road and make a smaller road, or maybe even two narrow paths, like what a wagon might roll on. Small, easy to make, and we could do a section each day, if we have enough people. How far away is the other place?" he asked.

If I answered his question, it would be a leap of faith on my part. Since he didn't know about my 'bots, I decided to tell him of the nanobots in my blood, what they did, and where they came from. The risk was worth the reward.

"The road surfaces to our east, and I'll want to connect the hidden spring where Derin and Scoot are set up. That's less than a klick. That comes first, before anything else."

Breslin squinted into the growing darkness. "Not much to work with, but okay. Four days, maybe five if we have water, my tools, and enough existing material."

"Five days. Not bad," I said, and I meant it. Building a network of roads—which was, in effect, rebuilding the modern world—was nothing short of a heroic task. "Let' me see if I can speed things up."

"How so?" he asked.

"Easy. More hands." I stood and walked to the center pit, jumping up on a tall rock that served as a table. "Everyone get enough to eat?" I asked. The answering cheer was music to my ears. We were well-fed, happy, and tired from productive work. For now, we avoided the bullshit of petty issues, but I knew those would come later. Right now, survival was still uncertain, and that went a long way toward eliminating things that didn't really matter.

"What do you need, boss? We got a belly full o' snake. This is the time to ask," someone shouted. It earned a good-natured laugh, like a warm ripple through the crowd.

"Right to the point, hey? Well, here it is. This big guy is Breslin, and he's going to take over two projects for us. Projects that will help us live in a way like, well—like these lights." I pointed over-head to the chain of bright white bulbs above our heads. They cast little pools of safety and civiliza-tion, and their light was steady and warm. Andi had a good connection, and the reactor was running perfectly.

"What projects?" Mira asked. She was sitting cross-legged, chewing idly on a stem.

"Water channels. Five of them at minimum, and the four new springs, and all that entails. They'll be covered, at least partially, by the baked tiles that Lasser's crew has been making. Breslin will run with that, so that's one part of what he'll oversee. The other is a bit more aggressive. We're going to use the highway exposed by the storms, and we're going to reconnect our points of interest. Here, Derin's new place, all the way to the Fortress. We need as many hands on this as possible. I'm not going to lie. It's hard work, but if you go to the road crew—or the waterways—we'll finish your house for you. I need three teams of as many people as I can get, and we'll start tomorrow. Show of hands?"

A forest of arms went up.

"I need twenty people to stay here for house construction, ten to feed us, and two for water. Other than that, security is covered and I'll start hunting hog tomorrow. We eat pig every night until the roads are done."

The answering cheer was loud enough to make me wince. It was amazing what good barbecue could do to motivate a group of hardened survivors.

"I'll take that as a yes. Mira, you're with me at dawn. Lasser is fishing, but when he returns he's second in command. Silk, you're in charge here, and everyone else, split up according to your skills. Kids stay put or run water. Derin and Scoot, you stay on task at your place—where's Beba?" I asked.

"Here," came a clear voice. I saw a graying head in the dim light.

"People are going to get dinged up on these jobs. As of now, you're our doctor. Are you good with that?" I asked.

She stood, an older woman who was still hale. "It's what I'm here for. I'll hang a sign. If anyone gets hurt, come to me. I have supplies and cane liquor."

"I think I'm hurt already, doc," came a voice from the crowd. The raucous laughter took a moment to fade, even after Beba patted the air with her hands.

"I need to see the wound before you get the drink. Don't think I'm a pushover. Work hard and you might get a drink anyway," she said to another round of applause.

"Guess we better set up a still," I said.

"I can do that," came a male voice from my left.

"Your name, sir? Stand up so we can see what a true hero looks like," I told him.

"Colaber," he said. He stood, smiling slightly. He was short, thick, and bald, with a hint of Asian features under his suntanned skin. His dark eyes glittered with good humor. "I have a still. Or most of one, I should say. I can produce cane liquor, root liquor, or even fuel if you need it."

"Let's start with something as a reward for hard work," I said. "How long would it take?"

"Give me a few days for the rough stuff, but something a little smoother would be ten days or so," Colaber said. His voice was mild and confident. "If I have a cool place to stash some bottles, then we can make something worth drinking."

"I'll see that you have that cool place and more. Get with Silk about supplies and location, okay? We have two small solar trucks that can carry enough gear to get you cooking in a matter of hours, as long as everything is close to The Oasis. Do you need anything from elsewhere? You're our distiller from this point forward, if you want the job," I told him.

"I accept," Colaber said with a small bow. People around him started slapping him on the back, reinforcing my belief that no matter where or when you are, it's always good to make friends with the bartender.

5

BRESLIN WAS as good as his word, and the next day, I took him underneath into the facility. He whistled in appreciation at the general state of preservation, nodding as we went from room to room, ending in the greenhouse.

"Of all the things you could have shown me, a room full of plants was the last thing I expected," he said. The rich smell of life hung in the air, and water churned past us in the access tank that supplied our projects.

"It's a greenhouse, but that won't last. We're going to move a lot of this out of here. At least the food production. As to the saplings, they'll stay until we've covered this area with some kind of greenery," I said.

"Do you think that will really work? I know you're having some success, but—a desert? How will you hold back a desert?"

"It wasn't always a desert, and I have examples of this working." I waved him back up the stairs into the daylight, considering my next move. "How old are you?"

The question brought him up short, but he shrugged and answered. "Thirty or so. Not exactly sure."

Around us, people were moving with great purpose as they carried parts of wagons to the housing sites Breslin and I selected. We needed fewer wagons and more homes for now, so we were using everything we had to make up for a lack of lumber. I listened to the good-natured jeering as two men hoisted a wooden wagon panel up, using it as a wall. The houses wouldn't be uniform, but they would be safe and dry. For now, that was good enough.

"I'm two thousand years old, give or take a decade, and everything you consider Hightec is from my life. My people. My world, if you can call it that, since it's so different." His eyes narrowed, and I sensed his raw disbelief. "Let me explain how that's true. You're right to doubt me, but I'm not the only person who's that old. Andi is, too."

"Bullshit," he said, but there was no heat in it.

"Fair enough. I was, ah—found—by Mira and her sister, Bel, to the north and west. I was in a machine that kept me in a permanent state of sleep all those years. I have—I have machines in my blood that kept me healthy, and when I woke up, I had no idea that the world was now an echo of what used to be," I said.

He was quiet for a long moment, then he lifted his brows. "Let's pretend for a moment that I believe this story, okay?"

"Okay. I'm listening."

He turned to me, his eyes narrowed with intensity, but I didn't flinch or look away. There was no need. I was armored with the truth, no matter how bizarre it might seem to this man from the distant future. "I've seen cars and trucks, engines. Computers, even. An array of things. None of them even hint at keeping a person alive. In fact, from what I can tell, machines *kill* people more often than not."

"True. But the things in my blood are too small to see with the naked eye, and there are hundreds of thousands working right now. They're called nanobots, and they are the absolute future of humanity. Do you want to know?" I asked.

"Of course."

"Andi has them in her system, and she's my age. Mira and Silk do not, but they will, because I want them to be safe in this—this world. This left-over disaster that we made somehow by fucking with the nature of life and breaking it like a cursed mirror," I said.

He whistled low, then tilted his head. "I've seen how you look at Silk. And Mira. You're really going to—how do the machines get in their bodies?"

"By injection, directly into the bloodstream. We have a medical facility that can do it—properly, and at the right ratios."

"And what happens?" he asked.

"Diseases are limited, or outright gone. I heal faster. I *am* faster, and stronger, and maybe a bit more decisive. Andi explained that the 'bots key into our strengths and develop them even more than nature could, which made me nervous because that's how we got all this," I said, waving around at the desert and all its horrors. "But no more. The 'bots are a means to drag humanity back from the edge, and we have them. We're going to stabilize the population, remove the shit that goes bump in the night, and build a city. Then we're going to build another, and after that, we'll build roads and waterways, too. Do you know how I know this is going to happen?"

Breslin said nothing.

"It's going to happen because I'll be alive to see it, if I'm not killed by some shitbird warlord or a— I don't know, a sand squid or some other tentacled horror that tears me apart in a fight."

"Is that like an octopus?" Breslin asked.

"Yeah. More tentacles. Ten, not eight," I said.

"No thanks. Saw an octopus in a river. If there are squid living under the sand, then I might have to live in a treehouse," he said with a sly smile.

"I might join you. The rattlers and hogs and scorpions are bad enough," I admitted.

We shared a quiet laugh, then his face grew serious again. "These—nanobots," he said, going slow with the new word, "they can help my kids survive? Longer, and with less sickness?"

"Yes."

He nodded. "Then I will at least listen. Jossi will, too." His face took on dark cast at the mention of his wife, but I ignored it. Family business was just that—for the family, and I was not a part of his.

I looked up into the night sky. Ever since waking up, I took every chance I could to see the stars. They were unaffected by cities and smog and anything else that humanity might have created, winking gemlike in an array of colors from horizon to horizon. A meteor flared to life south of us, and then it was just the Milky Way again.

"Are they the same?" Breslin asked.

"More of them, but, yeah. That's my sky." I stood, and Breslin followed. Around us, the dinner was breaking up as people found their places for the night. Silk and Mira were with Andi, looking at a light and pointing off down a lane, where they were doubtless planning to run the next powerlines. "I'll leave to hunt before dawn, but we'll be back by later afternoon. If you need anything at all, just ask."

"I'll show you what we can do tomorrow," Breslin said, and we shook hands.

"Judging by your arms, I'm betting it's a lot."

6

I NUDGED MIRA, whose eyes popped open immediately. "Time to bring home the bacon."

She smiled, her eyes bleary with sleep. Silk and Andi didn't stir, though I knew they would both be up shortly. When there's no city bustling around you, sleep comes easy, and you adopt a rhythm that your body considers natural.

"Mmm. Bacon. You just said one of the only things that will get me up before the sun," Mira murmured, putting her hair back in a leather thong.

We stood, moving quietly to the door. Our house was no bigger than the others, except for a small room on the back that served as an office and armory. There was a bed there, too, in case one of us needed alone time, though we hadn't used it yet. In a moment we were dressed and outside, standing next to the basin where we washed up. I handed her a towel while we brushed our teeth and then checked our weapons by hand. The first streaks of rose split the eastern sky, and somewhere overhead, a blood chicken squawked in protest. The day began, and we walked through the silent Oasis to the vehicle shed. The solar trucks waited, side by side and at full charge, courtesy of Andi.

"North, I think. We saw hog signs along that stack of bleached wood, you know the one?" I said, turning the key as we pulled silently away from the shed. The lane was wide, the ground dry, and when we came to the outer edge of homes a guard waved at us, alert and holding her rifle.

"Morning," she said in a musical voice. "Dinner hunt?"

"Hey, Shazz. Boys asleep? I thought they were stuck to your hip," I said, smiling. Her answering grin told me she, a mother of four young sons, was glad for the peace and quiet of a watch shift.

"Dead asleep. They chased lizards all day and got more sun than they needed." She wrinkled her nose at their youthful mistake, her own freckles and green eyes standing out on a light complexion.

"Nothing like a little chase to tire them out," Mira said. She liked Shaz. We all did. Her arrival a week earlier—along with her sons—had been something of a miracle, given their trek south from a defunct ranch that had been scoured clean in the storm. We were hearing that kind of story more than I liked, but I fully expected a steady stream of refugees once they learned of us. Especially given the savagery of the last storm season.

"We'll be back by afternoon. Who's relieving you?" I asked.

"One of those cowboys, the tall one with the long nose?" she said, uncertain.

"Vikez. He's a good shot. I'm sure he'll be right along." I started to pull away, waving goodbye.

"Save the feet for me. I'm going to pickle them," Shaz said as we drove off.

I made a face but dipped my chin to acknowledge her request. "She'll pickle anything, won't she?" I mumbled to Mira while accelerating.

"I think it's a mom thing. She's got four sons. They'll eat anything, and I'm not joking. They weren't chasing lizards for fun. They were chasing them to eat. Or . . . pickle." She shuddered, sticking out her tongue halfway.

"Pickled lizard?" I said, trying not to frown. "We really have become barbarians, haven't we?"

"If that word means unwashed animals, then yeah, but they're little boys. I think they're all like that."

"You like me, don't you?" I tried to leer, but it was a bit early, even for my libido.

She pulled at her lip as the desert sped by. "I might. *After* we bring down the hog."

I smashed my foot on the accelerator, and she laughed wildly into the sky. "That pig is as good as dead."

We spun quietly over the desert in companionable silence, and then, at some odd moment, we stopped being lovers on a day trip.

We became hunters.

"Sign," I said, squinting into the growing light. We were a full klick from the stack of bleached trees where I'd seen tracks a few days earlier, and even now, I could see fresh dirt turned up.

"Tuskmarks," Mira agreed. There were scars in the desert where the enormous hogs had rooted and torn for prey. Once they smelled an animal underground, they would stop at nothing short of digging a small canyon to pop it free. The feral hogs were opportunistic eaters, but then again, so were we.

"Walk it in," I said, rolling the truck to stop. We got out and unshouldered our rifles, checking ammo belts and knifes with the absent gestures brought about from practice. Mira moved like a wraith, while I stepped as lightly as I could at my size. My 'bots honed each sense to superhuman levels, and in moments, I smelled the distinctive odor of pig shit.

"Fuck me," Mira said a minute later. "They're such—"

"Pigs?" I asked.

Her smile was quick; her snort not very ladylike.

"If you make me laugh and give away our position, I'll develop a sudden case of lockjaw, and hips that won't move," she said, arching a brow.

"Understood." I pulled her up a small incline, then we both began to slither over the ground like eels. Below us, The Empty fell away, brutal and beautiful all at once. We were 200 meters from a crazy jumble of broken trees, bleached to bone white. The wooden mass caught my attention as both potential building materials and a nexus for prey.

"There they—oh, what the fuck is *that* thing?" Mira asked. She was looking away, near the end of the long pile of debris. The trees were stacked ten meters high by the stormwaters that had gutted the area. The animal that lurked behind them was three meters at the shoulder and moving fast.

Right toward a trio of giant hogs.

"How do they not smell or see that thing?" Mira asked. The beast was in the open now, churning sand and grit with each driving kick of its clawed feet. It was six meters long, thickly built, and bulging with muscles under a thin coat of mottled brown fur. It had—

"Horn?" I said, mostly to myself. "Wait, horns. It's a big bastard. Looks mean as hell."

"I've never seen anything like it, not alive anyway. Saw a skull kind of like that in the relics that some merchant in Kassos kept. Said it was a fossil. Something about—"

"What the *hell*. It's not a regular rhino," I said.

Mira turned to look at me in bewilderment. "What? A rhino?"

I grunted, never taking my eyes off the beast as it stopped to glare with eyesight that looked to be less than spectacular. "Rhinoceros was from my time, but in Africa, over the ocean. *That* big fucker is a wooly rhino, but with a light coat of fuzz. They died out long before civilization came on the scene."

The rhino began to paw the earth, its shoulders tensing for a charge. The hogs whirled and stood shoulder to shoulder, their own tusks lowered in a menacing display of ivory that shone in the rising sun. The scene felt like I was watching a nature show filmed in hell.

"The big one is going to turn them into paste," Mira said.

"Agreed." My rifle slammed a second later, and the closest hog fell over with a squeal. I wasn't going to let a prehistoric beast turn our barbecues into bloody mud. No matter how badass the razorbacks were, they didn't stand a chance against a creature the size of a truck.

With horns.

My shot was the tonic the pigs needed. They lowered their heads even further and charged, two massive slabs of ham with nothing to lose and attitude for days. Their low hindquarters shook comically as they accelerated away from us toward the rhino, who lowered its own horns and began to trot forward like a tugboat picking up steam. The space between them closed quickly, from a hundred meters to fifty and then ten.

Then the hogs split apart like wolves on the hunt, and the rhino bleated a cry of alarm.

"They're going to—" Mira said, then stopped because the three animals met, but not in the way the razorbacks intended.

The rhino dug in, slashing to the left with a horn that was a meter of brutal ivory, catching the closest pig in the jowl and hurling it skyward like a toy. But the rhino wasn't done, following through with a pivot that brought its hind end around in a flash, the hooves lashing out to catch the second pig in the ribs. Even at our distance, I heard bones cracking as the pig rolled sideways in a tremendous spray of sand and gravel. The rhino slid to a stop, whirled again, and proceeded to gut the second hog with a single, vicious cut of its horn, spraying viscera into the sky like a fountain.

"Seriously, that's gross," Mira said.

"Right. He did gut the pig for us, though. If he doesn't—oh. He's not done."

The rhino pummeled the corpses for a moment in a move of absolute superiority, then stalked off at a dignified trot that was neither slow nor fast.

The dead hogs lay steaming in the sun, their bodies broken, their hides worthless.

"Well, at least you shot the one," Mira said with a shrug.

"Let's take a moment and make sure that rhino puts a little distance between us. I don't want to try him, even with our rifles."

"You don't have to ask me twice," Mira said, pulling out a flask.

"Is that hooch?" I asked her, holding my hand out.

"Uh-huh. I brought some of that whiskey and a couple other things you might be interested in," she said, a wicked grin on her face.

"Like what?"

"These." She lifted her shirt. Her breasts were proud and glorious, and everything right with the world. "After we butcher the hog, of course. You know how bacon turns me on."

"That makes two of us," I said, sad that her shirt lowered but now highly motivated to skin that pig and tie it to the truck. Nothing makes a man work like proper incentives, I always say.

We waited and sipped the whiskey, and then we drove down to the kill zone. Up close it was even more gory, and for a moment I wondered if I had it in me to get naked with Mira that close to a meat market.

As it turned out, I did.

We skinned the hog and broke it apart, tying each huge section of meat to the truck and then covering it with a tarp. The heat was rising and we only had a few hours to get it to the fire, but we were only an hour's ride from The Oasis, which meant we had a surplus of time.

Mira took out wet cloths and wiped me down, then I did the same for her. She smiled up at me, her face a perfect mix of beauty and challenge. I touched a freckle on her honey skin, and her green eyes narrowed.

"Are you going to be romantic, or are we gonna let that hog spoil in the sun because you're being slow?" Her smile was brilliant, her lips full and inviting.

I leaned close, but didn't kiss her. Instead, I untied the heavy belt she wore, letting her pants fall to the ground. She was naked underneath, her skin tanned all over from years in The Empty. "I noticed, this truck is *just* about the right height."

Her brow went up as her hands went forward. Then my pants came down, and we both stood in each other's orbit, smiling at our good fortune.

When she took me in her hands, they were far from those of a woman who had to fight for every day. Her touch was soft, and in second, I was hard. I touched her, then ran my fingers along her inner thigh, folding back the delicate skin that was already heating from our desire.

"Sometimes I don't want to kiss either," she said, sliding forward and pushing down hard on every inch I had to give. It was slow going, and then it wasn't, as her will overcame her body's inability to keep up with what she wanted. She wanted us, together, pushing slow and holding tight under the blue sky.

I wanted the same thing, but her lips were too great an invitation. I kissed her, long and slow, and she kissed back like she was discovering me for the first time. Mira's edges were hard, but her core was softer than anything I'd ever known, and it was given only to me in moments like this. So, I was careful with it. Our tongues played, lazy and warm, and then I felt her clench around me with a need that made my vision swim.

It was a perfect kind of heat, standing there moving inside of her in the desert air. I took her dark blonde hair in my hands and pulled her up, then lowered her back on me with a push that took her breath away. And mine, too, as she nipped my ear with her teeth, breath coming in faster gasps that told me we were on the same page, and our chapter would be finished sooner rather than later.

"Now," she said, and I kissed her harder as she wrapped her arms around me hard enough to make my breath a chore. It was everything Mira was—fierce, honest, hot, and giving—and it was mine just then. I came as she did, lifting to the balls of my feet like I was straining to touch the one cloud that passed over us as we collapsed against each other, out of breath and smiling into each other's necks.

"Better every time. Almost like we learn," she mumbled, biting softly at my neck. Her tongue flicked out to taste the salt of my sweat, and then she did it again. I could feel the smile on her face as I faced the moment of withdrawal. It felt like the end of a perfect vacation, that Sunday before you go to work when the scenery is perfect but your dread is building with each hour closer to the end.

I pulled out, and she frowned, then kissed me again. "We're not doing that enough."

"No argument here," I told her. Then, with a gallant bow, I pointed to the truck. "Would milady like to drive or hold down the giant dead pig?"

"I think I'll drive, but the other option is tempting. You really know how to spoil a girl," she said, her green eyes glittering in the sun.

We drove back, and in the afterglow of Mira I began to wonder about the rhino, and the general state of animals since the virus.

And then I knew.

"We need to talk to Andi when we get back," I said.

Mira turned to look at me from the seat. "Bit late for a threesome, but, hey—"

"Not that, although I'll hold you to it. I think I know what happened to this place."

"This place?" Mira asked, a tiny frown on her face.

"The Empty. The world. All of it. The virus didn't just work one way, by splitting humanity. It split animals, too, but not just forward. I think it brought them back. From the past, and the only way to know is to dive into the Cache system."

Mira was quiet for a moment, then she asked a question in a small voice. "Weren't there giant— things? That lived long ago?"

I thought of fossils. I considered the rhino. "Like you can't imagine," I said, and her frown went deeper still.

7

We returned in late morning, hours ahead of schedule and loaded with dinner. A group of teens greeted under the careful eye of Natif, who acted like a small but effective general as he herded the kids into a line. In moments, the hog was gone, whisked away to the nearby smokehouse.

"It's too small," Mira said.

"That hog weighs as much as the truck, give or take a bit," I said in mild alarm.

"Not the pig. The smokehouse. We need another, and five times the size. With rows and multiple rooms. A place to process meat for the center of town, so to speak. Then we can build more as we go out, and one for fish, too, so it doesn't stink the place up." She made a face and I nodded in agreement. It was the best kind of planning to do things *before* we needed them.

"Okay. It's done. We could always go back to where we were today. A lot of wood out there, if we can find time—and enough hands—to shape it."

"I think that will be under control soon enough. That tall guy, the one who looks like he smelled something bad?" Mira said.

"Danto. Doesn't talk much," I said. He'd arrived a few days earlier and had been a sour presence everywhere he went. He was tall, lean, and gloomy. "He might need a purpose."

"He has one. He was a sawyer, back north. Worked a mill that ran on water and some electricity. Cut everything from pine to softwoods for the traders up that way. He's the guy to run it, but you'll have to talk to him. I don't like being around him, and no one else does, either."

"I hadn't realized he was that disliked."

"Not disliked. There's just this mood around him that I can't put my finger on. He's alone, too. Didn't come with a wife or kids or even a friend, far as I know," she said, as if this alone was enough to make him suspicious.

"I'll have a quiet word with him, see if a job

helps his attitude. If not, we ship him off with the traders. Sound good?" I asked.

"Good." She kissed me and began walking off, shouting at Natif to clean out the truck or she would do terrible things to his hide.

"Okay, Danto. Let's see if you want a job or a free ride," I said to myself, walking toward the center. There was a buzz of activity as it was nearly lunchtime, though I didn't see Breslin's giant form anywhere among the crowd.

Lasser waved as I walked up, his long face red from effort. "Lot of tiles today. I've got ten of us on forming. We'll need twice as many if we're going to keep up with the bull you found."

"Breslin?"

"The same. He's got his crew working like a tornado is on the way, and he's doing half of it himself. Never seen a single man dig that much, that fast. Like an armadillo, but taller," he said with a laugh.

"He's better company than a 'dillo, too."

"I'll say. Beba is working to clean up the kids. Says they've got dirty teeth and cuts and rashes, and she's not going to be happy until every one of them is in perfect health. She's got them scrubbing to the bone in a channel. I think some of the kids went in brown and are coming out pink, and if she isn't happy with their efforts, she has a brush that she's using. After the first kid howled his way through her scrubbing, all the rest went at their skin and nails like they were trying to wear them away," Lasser said, grinning broadly.

"A highly motivated group, it seems."

"Truly. So are mine. They're working well, and they understand that the sooner the tiles bake, the sooner we become more secure. With every two hundred tiles we can extend the channels ten meters in each direction, five in all. I'd like to say we can do more, but the water won't stay above ground for that long," Lasser said.

"What about ponds? Small ones, round? Use them for storage when you can't push the channel any farther."

"I—you know, that works. We can have smaller homes near the ponds, if not the channels. I think that will do it. Let me get with Breslin and confirm, so we can make tiles that will go around the basins," Lasser said.

"Let me know," I said, and he waved as he ambled off, his long legs taking him across the path with ease. "Now, let's see the log guy."

I found Danto working, which was a good sign.

He was taller than me by a couple inches, lighter, and wiry with the kind of frame that indicated a hard life. In another time, he'd fit the profile of a herdsman, but now, he was just a sullen, dark presence, his black eyes flashing with irritation as I walked up to him.

There were two ways to go about engaging with him, and I chose the method that kept any disagreement quiet and out of public sight. There was nothing to gain by being an asshole, and frankly, we could use his skills. I stuck my hand out and smiled. "Danto, I have a proposition for you."

He stared at my hand, then shook it reluctantly. "Yeah?" His voice was low and reserved, like he hated speaking.

"I won't bore you with a speech about teamwork or bullshit like that. I understand you're good with a saw, and you know your way around a mill. We need a mill. I'd like you to build it and run it."

His brows shot up on a face that was thin and sour. With a rough hand, he rubbed slowly at his scalp. There were small, bright scars among the black hair. Life had been hard for him, and whatever he expected to hear from me, it wasn't a job offer.

"I don't like taking orders," he said.

"I don't like giving them." We stood while he digested that, then he frowned in a new and interesting way, adding yet another unpleasant expression to his face.

"Why do you need lumber?" he asked. His tone was still wary, if not hostile, but I wasn't done with my pitch.

"To build the cities."

"*Cities?*" he asked, incredulous. Then he snorted and went back to scraping the piece of hide he was working on. His motion was practiced and careful. He was used to hard work, and skilled work, too. "Good luck. A city is a drain that collects trash."

Ah. There it was. I had an idea about what made him tick, so I lowered myself to a crouch, getting close enough to speak so only he could hear me. Kids were carrying tiles past us under the tree cover, but they paid us no mind other than some smiles and waves. We were effectively alone.

"How did you get those scars?" I asked.

He froze, and when he looked up, the sour expression was now unfiltered rage. "None of your fucking business."

"That's fair. How about if you hear my theory before I throw your ass out of this place?"

He dropped the hide, hands clenching into fists, but I ignored it.

"You got those scars from one of the elites in Kassos. Probably some asshole who fancies himself a lord or count or whatever they call themselves up there. He saw your skill, recruited you, and wanted you to work for free. In my time we called that slavery, and you took offense, so he had something done to you." I peered closer at the scars, then nodded. "Who put the beating on you?"

Danto was rigid with anger, but he managed to grind out a single word. "Faustas."

"Ahh. New to me, but not for long, I think. Is Faustas some kind of enforcer for . . . ?" I let the question hang. He was compelled to answer.

"Sipulvon." He hawked and spat, his eyes flat with remembered anger.

"I'm not Sipulvon." I waved around us. "Nobody here is anything like Sipulvon, or Faustas. Except for me."

His eyes shot up to meet mine, and I nodded slowly.

"You're no Faustas."

"Oh, I know. But there's a small part of me that is perfectly capable of that kind of violence. In fact, I'm built for it. Rebuilt, you might say. I'm not entirely human, and I can do things that would make Faustas shit his pants if he had any sense, but he doesn't, and I do, and that's why we're *building* cities instead of ruling over a failing ruin. Do you understand, Danto?" I asked him, my tone level.

"I'm not your fucking dog."

"And I don't want you to be. I want you to be yourself, and I want you to run the sawmill so we can stop people like Faustas from ruining lives. You don't have to like me. You don't even have to respect me. But you *do* have to agree with what's happening here," I told him.

"Which is what? A labor camp for you and your whores?"

My fist connected with his jaw, knocking him flat. I lifted him up so that we were eye to eye. "You fucked up, friend. You can insult me, but as for them—" I shrugged, grinning. I wasn't angry. I was making a point. That was the difference my 'bots made. What would have started a fight merely ended one now, as my emotions were completely in check.

He glared at me but said nothing.

"I don't give a shit if you approve of—well, anything. I don't have time for your archaic bull-shit. To repeat: I need your skill, and I can offer you something you want. Something no one else can give you."

"What's that?" he said, pulling away from me.

I let him go. He touched his jaw, but never took his eyes off me. That was good.

"I can give you Faustas, and eventually, Sipulvon. Hell, give me a *list* of the tyrannical assholes in Kassos, and we'll get around to each and every one of them. See, Kassos isn't going to last, not on my watch. Wetterick's Outpost is first, but I'm going to dismantle their little kingdoms one at a time and replace them with something they need."

"Another warlord?" he said, his voice rich with disgust.

"No. Freedom. Their place, their choice— within limits. Slavery is gone. Ogres won't be kept, nor will humans, nor any other species I haven't seen yet, and I don't think I've even scratched the surface of this place. There won't be women and children in chains, or men used as blade fodder, and the bandits that haunt the trading routes are in for the last terrible surprise of their lives. That's what I'm going to bring them. You understand?"

He considered that, his face mulish but softening just a little. "I heard there was a massive logjam where you killed that hog. I need it."

"The whole thing?" I asked.

"Every stick. I need access to a channel of water, too, and some hands to help. I also need to be left alone. I don't like you, and I don't like your —society."

"You don't have to. You'll have what you need, starting tomorrow. You can access the solar trucks, too, as long as Lasser goes with you. If you get out of line with him, you're through. Clear?" I asked.

He didn't answer, but he nodded, and that would have to do.

8

THAT NIGHT, I lay next to Silk, telling her the details of Danto and what I thought was going to happen next.

"I think the time for another power source is *now*, not later, and we may as well consider a second site," I told her. We were in bed, listening to a few people outside as they talked and planned for the coming day. The fire was still going, casting an occasional flicker through the two large windows on the front of our house. Andi and Mira were with the people, talking, bonding, and generally finding out how things were progressing. I was learning to delegate, and the results were excellent. My family was made up of exceptional people, and

The Oasis belonged to them as well. It made sense that they should be seen as part of our leadership.

Silk dragged a finger over my chest, idly. "A second town? That's what you mean, right?"

"It's inevitable, but we don't have people yet, and I'm not comfortable giving that kind of technology to someone who is unproven. I don't want to build a network only to have us fall apart in warring city-states at the first disagreement. That's bad for everyone, most of all whoever tries to seize power, because then we have to take them out."

"There will always be someone who disagrees. The key is making everyone participate. If the people have a reason to care, they'll take an active hand, and we can hold off warlords for a generation. Maybe two. But they *will* appear. It's the nature of men. And women," she added.

"Will you be a benevolent dictator?" I asked, laughing and rolling to face her. Her eyes were bright in the dim glow from outside.

"Naturally. You will come to love serving me, washing my feet and combing my hair as I carry on with world domination and—what was the term you used in the past, when I complained about the general lack of privacy we have for sex?"

"Empress, I believe," I said, recalling our

conversation. She'd been irritated that we could not find quiet time. Ever, it seemed.

"Perfect. Well, *this* empress—and Mira too, because she's still shy about her body—will construct a—something. I'm not sure what, but—"

"A love palace?" I asked, helpfully.

She touched my nose with a fingertip. "Exactly. There will be a bed, and bath, and none of those," she said, looking to the large windows with disgust.

"I'll build it for you, though it seems like a terrible waste of resources just so you can get laid in peace."

"Does this seem like a waste?" she asked, cupping my balls and pulling lightly with her fingertips. I felt the breath leave my body for an instant, like a spirit had passed through me. My natural reaction was instantaneous. Also, I began to caress her breasts because they were within range and I'm no fool. I waited 2000 years for that kind of opportunity, and I'd be damned if I wouldn't take it whenever I could.

"I spoke to Danto today," I said, trying to remain casual.

"Is that so?" Her hands never stopped moving.

"A hard man."

"That makes two of you," Silk said. I could

hear the smile in her voice. Her touch grew firm, then light, then firm again.

"I got my point across, but he needs supervision and proper motivation, despite his wish to be left alone."

"I'm a natural at supervision," she purred. "I'll see to it that he receives only the firmest of hands when it comes to keeping him in line."

"I'm sure you will." I kissed her then, because that was far more interesting than talking about some surly woodworker.

When we broke apart for air, her teeth were gleaming in a satisfied smile. Her hands slowed, but my fingers still flicked over her nipples, and then lower, earning a soft gasp. Maybe it was time to stop talking about problem employees. I slipped a thumb inside her and pushed it up and back, feeling the ridges of her innermost places. She bit my neck and flattened to me, her body soft and warm and writhing.

It didn't take long for her to come, and she let it happen in a series of clenches around my fingers, now split and working in two places at once. When she finished, I felt the twitch of memory as her hand began moving again, bringing me back to a level of hardness that was almost painful.

"Be right back," she said, lowering herself. A second later, her mouth slid down my shaft. Her tongue moved twice, then she pushed herself down until her nose touched my stomach.

I came hard and fast, with no apology or warning, and she let her mouth linger for a moment, sliding off me with a suction that was perfection itself.

"I hate making a mess," she said, lying back down with a grin.

It took me a moment to speak. "I'm glad you're such a clean freak."

"I am. It's one of the things an empress must be, or so I'm told."

"A third of my kingdom is yours," I told her, and she laughed, turning to put her face on my upper arm. Her body was light, her hair spilling across the blanket in a tangle.

We stayed quiet, listening to each other breathe as the noise outside began to fade. People were going to bed, because the work was hard and the sun rose early. Not for the first time, I found a silver lining in the fallen world. The sun dictated how we lived—for now, until we had more lights, and cities.

I felt a pang of regret that I would rewire the world, but it was too dangerous for humanity to live in the dark all the time. There were monsters now, and if unchecked, they would tear the last person apart given the chance. My family and I would have to be the gatekeepers against that happening.

"I have something to ask you, and it requires thought," I said.

"More thought than I usually give?" she asked. Silk was nothing if not careful, so she lifted herself to an elbow and watched me, waiting for the question.

"Do you want 'bots?"

The question hung for a moment, then she nodded. "Yes."

"Okay," I said, and like that, it was done. I knew Mira would follow suit, and a subtle tension left my body as I realized I'd been thinking about the issue for some time. Since the moment Andi told me she had access to nanobot treatment at the Cache, probably.

"Do you want to know why I said yes?" she asked.

"I do."

"Three reasons, in no order." She held up a hand and began listing the reasons for her answer, tapping a finger for emphasis with each thought.

"A longer life, and more chance to build something. More time with you and the girls."

"That's only two," I reminded her.

"Oh, the third is easy." She took me in her hand and began stroking again. "I'm not going to be done with you for a long time."

9

THE SUN WAS WELL UP when Breslin introduced me to his wife.

"Hi, Jossi," I said, shaking her hand. She had strong hands for someone so small. A tiny blonde woman, she was cloaked in nervous energy, eyes darting around as she met me. There was an evasiveness to her that made me think she was ready to run away at any moment, but then her kids came up in a friendly tumult and she calmed down, if only slightly.

"Hi. Jack." She continued to look up at me, pale blue eyes squinting in the sun.

"Tell him your plans, dear," Breslin said, beaming at her. He dwarfed her in every way, but almost seemed deferential in bearing as he stood

73

next to her, holding his battered hat in a giant hand. "I'm off to the new channel. We're blocking in another pond this morning. There will be room for five around it."

"Houses or craft stalls?" I asked.

"Either. Good sized pond in a natural depression. It'll be a meter deep at the edge and two in the middle. Not a bad place to put fish, if you ask me," he added.

Jossi frowned.

"Not a fan of fish?" I asked her, trying to lighten her mood.

"Not really, but I guess they're better than ducks. Noisy things," she said with a shake of her head.

"She doesn't like messes, really. I'm off, then." He bent to kiss her cheek, and she tilted up to him, if only just. "Back later."

He strode off, bellowing to his crew, who were taking advantage of the break to grab food from the community table. I was left with Jossi and a hum of discomfort, so I broke it with an obvious question.

"Breslin says you make paper?" I asked, inviting her to speak.

She nodded, her lips tight, but then something

loosened around her mouth and she looked directly at me. "And fabric, too. I can dye things, if I have anything to work with. Some of the things we made came from rags, but when you dye them, no one knows."

"Knows what?" I asked.

"That my children are wearing trash. It's colorful, but it's still trash."

"I'm sure you did the best you could," I said.

"Mm-hmm," was her answer. She looked away, watching their children tussle with a large section of wood to be used for the firepit.

"Would you like a shop? We're not always going to be a barter community, and at some point in the near future, your business would be your own."

"What do you mean?" she asked, the light of interest in her eyes.

"Money. Your own money, and earned with a skill only you seem to have, at least for now. As to the people who show up today, and tomorrow, I don't know. But for now, it would be just you making paper and fabric work. We could pick a site for you near the pond that your husband is tiling in, unless you want to work close to your home?" I asked. Their home was to the left, on the main channel and less than a hundred meters from mine. The site was already shaded by trees that were leaping upward, the product of seeds that had been tweaked to grow at unnatural rates.

"Away is better," she said quickly. When I raised a brow at her response, she added, "Dye work stinks. Paper work isn't much more fragrant."

"Ahh, right. So away, then. Maybe out at the edge, where the new springs are?"

"That would be—that would be good," Jossi said. "Thank you." The words sounded odd, like she was unused to being considered in decisions, though Breslin gave no signs of being a tyrant whatsoever.

"I'll have Silk help you pick the site," I said. "May I ask you something about your husband?"

She looked alarmed, then her eyes narrowed. "Okay," she said in a neutral tone.

"How did you meet?"

Whatever she'd been expecting, that was not it. For nearly a full minute, Jossi stood, forming her answer. I've found that when people take time to respond, it either means they want to be accurate, or they're full of shit and a lie is coming forth.

Jossi was unreadable when she answered. "In Kassos. I was young."

"Were you free?" I asked, pressing.

"Yes," she snapped with a toss of her head. "I was no slave. I—worked. I made clothes, for a large house. Good clothes, too, not the shit my children wear." She looked down at her own shirt and pants, hanging on her small frame. "Or I wear."

"I didn't mean to offend, just curious." She was mollified, but only somewhat. Her eyes still flashed with anger, and it was directed at me. I tried something different. "Your children are safe here, Jossi, no matter what they wear. And they *will* have better things, starting with your own craft stall and home."

She considered that, then nodded once. "Thank you."

At that moment, a raptor screamed and dived, swooping through the trees with its toothsome beak open as it streaked toward a clump of children.

Jossi stood frozen, but I didn't. I drew my gun and fired in a smooth motion, spattering the predator's skull in a cloud of blood and bone. It hit two branches on the way to the ground, spiraling wildly before thudding into the sand less than five meters from Jossi's children.

"Someone take it to the fire for dinner," I barked, sliding my rifle back into place.

"Safe, huh?" Jossi asked, her voice raw with accusation. She stared at the dead thing, its beak filled with razor teeth. The top of the skull was gone, as well as the odd purple wattle on its neck. One of the feet twitched spasmodically, and Jossi shuddered in response to the creature's death rattle.

I had nothing to say, bathed in Jossi's anger. After two kids carried the dino-bird away, I scraped at the bloody sand with my boot. "Get with Silk. She'll help," I said, not looking at the Jossi, who still regarded me with naked suspicion.

"I will," she said, then turned away without a word. I glanced at her as she stepped away, wearing her loose clothes and a frown. Unlike me, Jossi could not see the potential of our world. I hoped we could change her mind, if only for the sake of her children and Breslin.

10

THE SUN WAS high when Andi came to me, holding her tablet and frowning.

"What's up?" I asked.

"Power. A second reactor, to be exact. I have a site, and we have the need. It's time," she said.

"Tell me where." I leaned against a stump. We were near the firepit, and around us activity was reaching a daily peak, when everyone was tired but looking forward to the end of work.

"Here." She pointed to her tablet, where she'd drawn a map of our settlement, and then a larger map that showed the Cache and every water source we had found in the past month. To the east, there was an expanse of land that had two water sites, no massive gullies, and room to grow.

"It's perfect. One problem."

"Security?" she asked, looking up.

"Yes. It almost requires a second population from the beginning to insure that we don't invite disaster. Losing a reactor is one thing. Losing people is another. I don't know enough about the area to say there isn't a rogue tribe over the hill, so to speak."

She smiled, and I knew she was one step ahead of me. "I have a solution to that little issue."

"I'm all ears."

"The Vampires," she said.

"Huh." I thought about it and knew she was right. "What's their max altitude?" They were glorified gliders, but light and powerful enough to get us aloft. As to their range, I had no idea. We were holding them back for a rainy day, like the mustang and the weapons cache.

The sky was clear, but it may as well have been raining.

"A thousand meters without a mask. Three thousand with, and I have something that will kick our recon range up drastically. A Condor," she said.

"The drone? How can it—oh. Mount and launch from the Vampire?"

"Yep. It gives us an eye in the sky up at seven thousand meters, minimum. Maybe eight if we catch a current." Andi's eyes glittered with the possibility of using tech that could give us actual security. We had an enormous number of items at our disposal, but no way to keep them safe in The Oasis. High altitude recon could change that. We would know who our neighbors were—if we had any at all.

I stood away from the tree, brushing bark from my hands. "How soon can we leave?"

Andi whistled, high and shrill. Natif came running with her go-bag. "I'm already packed."

We said our goodbyes and left in a truck, determined to arrive at the Cache before dark. Given the predators in and around the site, it was in our best interest to be fast.

We hauled ass.

Following the highway remains, we struck east and then north, making excellent time and seeing nothing more menacing than a gathering of blood chickens that had brought down some kind of steer, its body opened up to the failing light of day as we swept past at forty klicks an hour. Before dusk could get serious, we saw the Cache grove and silos, their familiar shape rising as we sped up the path that had once been a hunting trail for marauding scorpions. There would be no more invasions of the Cache thanks to our hard work and good doors; we had the place buttoned up tight in case any random scavengers thought to go on a gear hunt inside our stash.

"We can park right near the doors," I said, letting us drift to a stop. Andi agreed, jumping down and pulling her tablet out to key in the unlock sequence. We didn't rely on anything as plain as a metal lock. Andi used a remote code to throw the huge bolts back, letting the door swing open on silent hinges.

The air inside was fresh. Andi had a circulation system working on cycles, so that the massive array of gear, printers, and weapons would remain dry and free of corrosion brought on by wind and water.

"Smells brand new," she said. "Those evap units are doing the trick."

"And then some," I said, running a finger over the wall. It was dry as a bone and cool to the touch. Out of habit, I drew a pistol as Andi lit the place up. Along the stairwell and halls, lights flared to life in a warm hue, their low hum a welcome noise after the unnerving silence of The Empty and our hissing tires.

"I need to go to Control first," Andi said, pointing herself down the stairwell.

"After me." I started down the metallic stairs, gun ready. The scents of decay and animal nests were gone. The Cache was alive with purpose instead of predators, and we were standing before Control in seconds. Andi swiped her tablet and the door opened obediently. She swiped her tablet again, and the massive screen flicked to life, as well as a series of terminals and lights. The room was brilliant with reminders of a world that had been gone for a long time.

But we would bring it back.

"Send up a Condor in a lazy eight, and then we can talk about dinner," I said.

Andi nodded her agreement and began keying in the commands for a drone launch from one of the silos. There were drones stationed at the top of each, and a plexiglass hood slid back above us, freeing one of the large drones to launch itself when the wings unfolded into a locked position. In ninety seconds, the Condor was aloft and sending data, an aerial picture of the Cache spread across the screen before us with wind, distance, and threat vectors spooling along in the right corner. To the north, a massive lizard waddled toward a Creekside den, its pace slowing as torpor overtook the animal.

"Cold-blooded," Andi said, staring at the image of the lizard.

"Enlarge his pic for me?" I asked.

She did, and when the beast turned to look back at something, I could see a smear of gore on its muzzle. "Not cold. Full. Been eating good."

Andi winced, then moved the drone to scan where the animal was looking. A dozen blood chickens and some other scavengers swarmed over the remains of a fresh kill, squabbling in a mass of beaks and talons as the sun went down on another lovely example of Mother Nature being a stone-cold bitch.

"Glad we're in here," Andi said.

"Same. I've had enough lizards for right now. Loop the drone?"

"Done," she said, tapping her tablet in quick, confident motions. "Vampires before dinner, then schematics and training?"

"Good. Take me to the goodies," I told her.

She lifted a brow and popped her hip out. "So soon? But we've just met, good sir."

"Dirty girl. The weapon goodies first. I have plans for *your* goodies later."

"Finally, an idea I endorse. Been a few days," Andi said. Her sex drive was only slightly higher than her intelligence, which is to say, limitless. I high-fived myself mentally as we went downstairs again, emerging at the end of the hall near the second and *far* more interesting weapons depot.

"Hello, girls," Andi said. The Vampires hung on the wall, folded into compact units that assembled on command due to an array of nanobots. There were flying suits, masks, and arming brackets alongside, all in numbered sequences. We took two of each—I carried the Vampires, as they were a hundred kilos each—and started back up the stairs. My muscles sang with effort, but I was able to haul the units without trouble because my 'bots kicked into overdrive and Andi's pear-shaped ass was just ahead of me on the stairs as we went up. There's a lot to be said for proper motivation.

We hit the commissary, which had no food but everything we needed to cook, and while Andi got the training rep ready on her tablet, I made stew with pork and herbs, and we settled to eat as she pulled up a video of how I was supposed to fly without killing myself.

"Your 'bots are going to have a lot to do with this, because your reaction times are no longer really human. With that being said, you *can* die if you hit the ground at a hundred klicks," Andi warned.

"How would I be—oh. Terminal velocity?"

"Right. If you collapse the wing or fall out, which I've never seen before, but—" She shrugged. "You'll be cabled in for data, too."

"The suit is wired?" I asked.

"Yep. One connection, directly to the helmet. There's a heads-up display that works with eye movement, and I'll be in control of the Condor. The drone launches from my Vampire at maximum height, and we'll set it to mirror us at the greatest safe distance we can without losing direct data feed. It's going to record everything it sees."

"So, over the horizon for us?"

"And then some," she enthused. "We might get coverage out to—ninety klicks? Since our range is a hundred and fifty in any direction, easy, that means we're going to have a rolling sitrep all the way to Fort Smith, or maybe even Tulsa."

"What about Oklahoma City?"

She pulled at her lip, thinking. "Maybe. If I

could link to some of the permanent birds, I might—"

"You think there are satellites still in orbit?" I asked, stunned. Two thousand years was a *long* time for ruins to exist, let alone space tech at the edge of human capability.

"I wouldn't be surprised. The bigger birds that went up after you were in cold sleep had their own defense nets, and most had nuclear thrusters."

"You mean—they had weapons?"

"Not *just* weapons. Other satellites in stable positions. We called them lambs. In the event of a kinetic attack, the lambs gave themselves up until the main bird could shift orbit with its thrusters. We were battling with the French and Chinese for orbital space, but it was the private firms who *really* crowded the skies. Heavy lift rockets were so cheap that private corporations could afford to launch spy birds for industrial espionage, and before you ask, there was a healthy business of countermeasure launches. Companies could launch on Monday and have their satellites torn to junk by an outbound drone strike less than a day later. It was utter chaos. The only really stable networks were in high orbit, and that took a lot of money. Government money."

"Can you search for an uplink from here?" I asked.

"I already did, but we need to print another antenna. The Cache network link was torn away sometime in the past three hundred years, given the break in data. This facility has been collecting info for seventeen centuries. We can watch it on a loop, if you want. It's like—it's like seeing the world die."

"Play it," I told her. Since I'd woken, the end of the world had always been in the back of my mind. I needed to know. I had to see.

She tapped her tablet, and for the next hour we watched the world die.

One city at a time, the lights went out. We saw dams fail, their floods taking people and towns with them, creating giant fans of sludge that colored the oceans, faded, and were gone. I saw fires a thousand miles across, and the telltale signs of war between surviving pockets of humanity as resources became scarce, leading to starvation and death on a scale the world had never seen. Buildings fell, highways buckled, and cities became inundated by water or covered by dunes. The planetary chaos only lasted a few years. After that, it was purely nature.

The earth reclaimed what it had given up.

Then, after a century, lights began to flicker back on here and there. We saw small cities bloom, grow, and die as people found ways to build again, but there was rarely anything that lasted for more than fifty years.

"The life of a strong leader," I said.

"One king or queen, and then chaos again. The cities fade back into obscurity due to the death of their throne. Or something like that," Andi said, pointing somewhere in South America.

"What the hell is—was—that?" I asked. There was a city, then lights, and then a glowing crater.

"Volcano, I'm guessing. Took the entire city with it. We never should have built around active peaks, but humans are stubborn. See that? Massive wave took that one. Looks like New Zealand held on to some kind of civilization, at least until an earthquake took them out," Andi said, her eyes saddened by an event that happened twelve centuries ago while we slept.

"I'm amazed that anyone made it at all, let alone built cities. Where did they find the tech?" I asked.

"I think it was handed down. I don't think the chain between old and new was entirely broken, and people were able to share oral history, and maybe some of what we knew. What we know, actually." She turned to me, thoughtful and grim. "There might be others out there, you know. People like us, still sleeping. I know I wasn't the only one, and I know I was kept away from the entire story. There might be whole rooms filled with sleeping engineers."

"I doubt it," I said.

"Why? Tubes were cheap. Hell, *engineers* were cheap."

"True, but you're forgetting human nature. It makes perfect sense to put doctors and engineers and scientists into the tubes, to wake up later and help reclaim the world from the virus and its shit-storm, but that's not what happened. At least, not on a large scale, I bet. Think about how fucking petty we were," I said.

Andi's face fell, and she lowered her head into her hands. "Oh, shit. You're right. There would be fucking politicians. Elites. *Lawyers*."

"Now you've got it. They would bribe or threaten their way in, which means that some-where out there are completely worthless people taking up space that could have been used by—

well, people like you. People we need, if we're going to succeed," I said.

"Sometimes I hate people," Andi said.

"Same here, but for now, show me how to fly the Vampires. I'm tired of watching a movie when I already know it ends badly."

She touched her tablet and the image changed to a schematic of the Vampires. "Let me introduce you to the Vampire Softwing Aircraft, also known as the GU-11. Ready?" she asked.

"Show me," I told her, and the images on the screen began to move.

11

WE TOOK the Vampires up to greet the dawn, setting the heavy bundles down on the expanse of silo roof. The air was still, and fresh with the oncoming day. I pulled the flight gear on, marveling at how it kept me at an even temp from the second I closed the gloves and zippered the neck.

The suit clung to me, but it was light enough that I didn't mind. Andi and I stood on top of the second silo, our helmets on and cable ready to plug into the Vampire's avionics system. Our air would come from a second tube, smaller and linked to a pressurized bladder along the frame. Nanobots would pump and compress oxygen as we went; the entire system had been designed after I was in cold sleep, and seemed nothing short of magical to my expectations.

"Condor ready. We can hit the assembly key. Here's how to do it," she said, showing me the sequence from her tablet. It was a simple flow chart, and when she touched the *Fly* icon, both Vampires began to inflate like parade balloons. In less than two minutes, they were firm to the touch, each wing spanning nearly six meters.

"This is fast," I said.

"Wait until you see the frame. It's harder than steel, but flexible when it needs to be. We built larger versions of these for long distance freight drops in remote areas. They could fly in, unmanned, deliver a payload, and return without any human supervision," Andi said.

"How long did it take before they were using them as air support?"

"About two seconds," she said wryly. The military would never let an opportunity for bombing go to waste, especially if you could avoid combat losses.

"Hook up here?' I asked, pointing to a cable mount on the front bar. I would step into the frame, and then when we were airborne, push my feet back to lock in place.

"Go ahead and hook up, then engage the camo," she said.

"Camo? Where?"

"Underneath. The 'bots act like the skin of a squid. We'll be invisible, more or less, and high enough that no one will see us. Our suits are linked to the camo pattern, and our Vampires are linked together. We fly unseen," she said.

My heads up display flared to life when I clicked the cable in place, and it was simple and bright. "Good HUD."

"It gets better, too." She took one side of the Condor and lifted. "Help me fit this?"

I lifted the other side of the drone and positioned it on the mounts just above center on her Vampire. The drone was light enough to avoid producing much drag, and its profile was so low that she would have no problem getting to the Vampire's full altitude. When the Condor was in place, she smiled.

"We speak into the mask. There's a wire mic in the lower edge. Ready?" Andi asked me.

"And then some."

"I'll launch first. Watch my feet," she said. She took three big steps and pushed away from the silo as a low whistle began.

"It's my engine kicking in," her voice said in my ear.

"Quiet."

"It pushes hard. Come on up. It's a heluva view," she said.

I took three steps, bunched my muscles, and leaped. I expected to fall for a second before the small engine kicked in, but I didn't. I began to climb immediately, and fast enough that my stomach dropped. In seconds I was wheeling away from the Cache to join Andi in her spiral upward, the tress and silos shrinking fast. Around me, The Empty sprawled in a rugged vista, dotted with scrub and cacti and broken rock of every kind. The highway—and now I saw two exposed sections, running north and east—was clearly visible. There was enough material to use for a passable track that would go well over the distant horizon.

"That's I-35 over there," Andi said.

The ribbons of highway dipped below sand and grit, emerging in sections long enough to tell where the original roadway existed. The storm gave us exactly what we needed to find and use a resource we would be hard pressed to recreate.

"Will our helmets pick all this up?" I asked.

"Every detail. We can even zoom in on the

upload. We've got room for two days of recordings, even though we can only remain aloft for ten hours at most. We're going to need a thousand people to build that road, minimum," Andi said.

"Baby steps. It's enough to know where it is, and then open it in sections. We'll go north and west to wherever the other locations are. I want such a surplus of gear that we'll never worry about technology again, and I want more printers," I said.

Andi banked, heading due east and continuing to climb. "Almost ready to launch the Condor. Better get alongside in case things go wonky," she warned. We were high enough that I could see a vast span of The Empty, revealing new, terrible gorges torn by the storm. Two of the gorge branches were so deep that the shadows hid their bottom when we flew over. They would require bridges if we were to build in this direction—which we would, but it would be years unless we found a source of people who wanted to join us.

"We're at launch altitude," Andi said. "Clear?"

"Clear. Send the bird," I replied.

Andi grunted and the Condor broke free from her Vampire, soaring up and away at a sharp angle. It began gaining altitude quickly, turning to follow us as it climbed at an astonishing rate.

"Does it have to be close for data transfer?" I asked.

"No, but I want us together for landing. We're going to cover a lot of ground. See that ruin?" she asked.

"Big. Looks like a single building, but huge." I sifted my memory of the area and drew a blank.

"Hospital. Looks like some of it survived underground. I'm dropping a pin for crews later," Andi said, and I saw her mark as a bright red point on my HUD. "You can drop them too. Just focus, blink three times, and it's marked."

"Got it. That river is new," I said.

"Was a creek twenty centuries ago, but The Empty and the rain fucked things up. Nothing is as it was in our time." Andi didn't sound bitter, just somber. We were seeing the death of our world from the air, and it was humbling.

"Where does the Eden Chain start?" I asked. I knew there were multiple sites, but I couldn't tell how close we were to the first marked site on Andi's digital schematic.

"Eighty clicks northeast is the first location," came her answer.

"Will we be able to see it?"

"We have the range to get close, but you wanted to go west as well. We can get in the area and check the Condor footage later, sound good?" Andi said.

"Perfect. Take us there, I've seen enough broken road to get a plan together for our eastern expansion."

We banked again, and the sun cascaded across the land, which began to change. "It's not as big as I thought," I said. The Empty was losing hold, as more and more cacti gave way to greenery of various kinds.

We flew on for ten minutes, the Condor high above and feeding us a steady stream of data and video. Its vantage was dramatically better than ours, despite my view being nothing short of incredible. I saw evidence of a world that had fallen, regrouped, and fallen again. Based on what we saw from satellite data, it was no surprise that the ruins were all over the timeline. The only thing missing were actual towns, although we flew over something that looked like bleached bones, and I recognized it as a collapsed log stockade nearly a half klick across.

I dropped a pin because the site was at a nexus

of two paths *and* it was close to the first legitimate stand of timber I'd seen in The Empty.

"Good call," Andi said.

"That's a ready-made outpost of our own, and the paths converge here for a reason. What it is, I don't know, but it's worth finding out someday," I said, following the paths away to the west and southeast. They were defined enough to be ruts, as if wagon traffic had packed them down over time. When we saw the shattered remains of an old cart, I knew my suspicions were right. "Trade route, and that means people were in this area within the past few years. Could the western track run to Wetterick's place, or even Kassos?"

Andi didn't answer, instead dropping a pin on a massive herd of horses. There were hundreds of them, running wild and free in the sun, their coats glistening with health.

They never saw the big cat waiting along their trail.

The cat burst out of cover, lunging at a dun-colored yearling, its mane flying as it cut hard to get away. The yearling shouldn't have bothered running, because an enormous stallion charged the cat, whirling to kick it square in the shoulder with hooves that looked to be the size of dinner plates.

The predator went down, rolled, and decided that discretion was the better part of valor, at least on this day. The stallion ushered his herd north as the enormous cat slunk away with a distinct limp.

"Let me say again; nature is an absolute bitch. How big was that cat?" I asked.

"Looked like a liger or some variant. Five hundred kilos at least. Those horses are huge, too. They looked like draft animals, but taller. Things aren't what they were when we got tubed, I'll say that." Andi's voice was full of wonder as we watched the horses streak west toward a ribbon of water.

"What's that?" I asked, dropping a pin for Andi to see. There was a depression in the land to our north, deep and irregular, but with straight lines.

Andi flashed the time in my HUD. "We can land and check it out, leave the Condor up. It's almost time to eat, anyway."

"Sounds good. Feet first, right?"

"Better than ass first. Follow my lead, flare the wing like in the training vids. You'll land like a feather. Promise," Andi said with a laugh.

We began our descent in a spiral, but not before checking the site for predators with a low-level pass. When we saw the site was clear, we flared our wings and touched down, soft as a feather. The small hydrogen engine whined to a stop in seconds, and I was struck by the utter silence.

"Seems quiet," I said.

"Everything is after that wind. Tires me out," Andi said. "And I have to pee."

"Glad you said it. I thought I was going to turn this flightsuit into a wetsuit, and not the good kind."

Andi laughed and began shucking her flight gear, then found a convenient stump to hide behind. I followed her lead and we rallied back together after pinning the Vampires to the ground with two stakes that descended from each wingtip. The Condor did lazy eights above us, and I held my pistol like a talisman.

Around us, the ground was unremarkable, except for the one thing that caught my eye from the air.

"Tell me what you see," I said.

Andi looked around, pushing her blonde hair back in frustration. "It's . . . well, it's big."

"It looks like the outline of that hospital you pinned. Same size, if you continue the walls. The shape. But it's buried, except for this side and part of that section that goes north. Same style, same setup. What do you think? Do you remember a hospital out here, in the middle of nowhere?"

"This was Oklahoma. It was *all* the middle of nowhere." She looked around, tapping a nail on her teeth. "You're right. What the hell would they build a hospital out here for?"

"Since you don't know it, maybe it was built *after* we went under," I said.

"Holy shit. We need to dig, maybe—something to confirm it," she said.

"And if it is, then it means that whoever ran it was practicing medicine *after* the virus broke out." The thought of all that data—and maybe treatments—was dizzying. I had no idea if the virus was dormant, or even if it had ever gone away, but I knew that nanobot treatment made a lot of sense if you were going to combat something that cracked life apart like an egg. What the virus left behind was nothing short of impossible, and yet here it was; animals from the deep past, things out of nightmares, and forms of humans who had been robbed of their dignity and lives.

"This is a huge place. We need help," Andi said.

"I agree, but I have a simple way to confirm it's a hospital."

"How?"

"Does our suit system have a Geiger counter?" I asked.

Andi smiled, then slapped her forehead. "Sure does. We assumed these suits would be used during all kinds of war, not just conventional." She blinked in rapid succession and began walking toward the center of the depression. When she'd gone a hundred meters, she stopped. "Rads below. Welcome to the department of nuclear medicine, sir."

"You may address me as doctor," I told her.

"You're no doctor," she said, grinning.

I touched her face, smiling. "Wait until tonight."

12

WE TOOK off after lunch and a good look around at the buried hospital. In open air, we could make ninety klicks an hour, but with a tailwind. We pushed well over a hundred, and still the Vampire wing held firm as the 'bots adjusted for pressure and stress. The Vampires were nothing short of magic, letting us wheel and dip all while collecting a running survey of lands that would be close to half of ancient Oklahoma, the Texas border, and points north. Other than natural predators, we'd seen nothing more menacing than a small group of prospectors who were reworking an ancient mine of some type.

They never saw us, and we didn't stop to chat. When we turned west for the final leg of our flight, we saw a series of small lakes that looked like a chain of gems, the mirror waters crowded with herd animals and greenery at the edges.

"Good looking land. How far to The Outpost from here?" I asked.

"It's sixty klicks north and west. I thought you said The Empty was peak desert?"

"It was. I think that storm knocked something loose with the local climate. This isn't nearly as grim as when I woke up. I'm seeing a *lot* of growth, and the animal herds are way too big to be desert dwellers. We were hunting rattlers and blood chickens for every meal. This is a totally different kind of landscape," I said.

"I'll patch us into the Condor and see how far north the changes are," Andi said.

She did so, and I had a moment of vertigo as my helmet view switched to the Condor's camera far above us.

In the distance, I saw a column of smoke.

"Andi, look."

"Got it, pulling the lens in. It's—shit," she said, her voice sour.

"I may be wrong, but that looks like a war party, and they're coming from The Outpost." Three wagons and a small hut were burning, sending black smoke skyward. I could see dots of people moving around, then the Condor lens focused again.

"Fuck me," I hissed.

Twenty men and women were in the process of staking a man to a pole. There were bodies on the ground, and as I watched, I saw a figure break free and run. A woman with black hair smoothly drew a rifle and shot the fleeing victim in the back. The body tumbled once and fell still.

"Raiders," Andi spat. "We could use a drone. One pass and they're dead."

"And heading south. Toward our place," I said, following their path. "No drone. I want one of them alive. I have . . . questions."

"How long have we got?" she asked.

"A day. Maybe two. Time to head back, I think. I need to greet our friends and take care of something I should have done a long time ago."

"Kill everyone in The Outpost?" Andi asked as we banked hard and began streaking south.

"Not everyone. Just the ones who don't want to join us, and I have an easy way to find out who they are."

We landed before sunset, breaking the Vampires down by command process and tucking them back underground. I decided to leave the second reactor for another trip since time was of the essence, and it was just getting dark when we got in the truck and rolled out, our thoughts turning back to war as we rode in silence.

"I should have done this some time ago. This is my fault," I said.

"What is?"

"The people who died. It's on me. We'll find out if there are any survivors after I'm done with those pricks. I have to decide if I leave one alive or not. I need to get the message out, but if they're murderers, I can't let them live," I said. I could hear the anger in my own voice, and I tried to dial back any unreasonable rage. Killing the raiders wasn't personal. It was business, and I had to remember that when the bullets were flying and people were screaming their last sounds.

"I don't want your default to be killing. That's not the man I want, and it's not what we need as a society. We need you, Jack, not a tyrant, and your natural desire to avoid being that is why this thing is working. It's why you have us." She rubbed at her scalp, then shrugged. "Your women, I guess. There's a phrase I never thought I'd be a part of, but you're not some knuckle dragging asshole. You use violence as a tool."

"Does this mean we're going steady?" I asked her, trying to lose my dark mood.

"I'd say so, given what we do to each other at every chance. Now clear your head and think about who and what we want to do this job."

"You, Mira, Silk, eight other guns, and Breslin. I want to see what he's made of," I said.

"Good call. Just because he's big doesn't mean he likes the rough stuff, though I have my suspicions he'll be a damn fine soldier when it comes to the fight."

"I'm with you. Tired?" I asked her.

"A little. That wind wears me out, but my 'bots are pulling me through. I'll be okay," she said.

"When we get back, you go home and explain. I'm going to get Breslin and the others. I want to meet these assholes well outside our outer perimeter. The farther they stay away, the better.

"I know you'll do what's right, Jack," Andi said. She leaned over and kissed me, then settled back in her seat, putting a boot out the window. The night air was cool in the cabin, and the windshield was filled with stars. We were driving without lights, since

I could see well enough and we didn't want to risk a scout seeing us approach. The Outpost wasn't known for producing brilliant minds, but I couldn't risk leading a war party right to our door in the dark.

When the first blaze of lights flared into existence, we turned on the headlight to let everyone know we were coming. After answering the guard challenge, we rolled in, parked, and set about assembling our defense.

This time, I swore, I would make my point, and then I would lay plans to break The Outpost apart and either bring them into our fold or eliminate them forever.

The choice would be theirs.

13

THE OASIS WAS ACTIVE, but not chaotic. That was due to my belief that losing your mind over something makes other people act in the same way, and that kind of frantic energy would achieve nothing.

I called everyone in for a central meeting—which made me realize we needed a communications network—and told them we had unwelcome guests on the way.

"I'm going to take a few of you with rifles, and the remainder will be organized by teams. This force is too small to take us," I said, not shouting, but in a firm voice over the low hum of concern from everyone around the firepit.

"I can be ready with bandages and clean water," Beba said.

"I was just about to ask you. They have guns, but they also have knives. Not that it's going to matter," I said.

"Why?" someone called out. It was a young man, somewhere at the edge of the group.

Silk stepped closer to me, and nodded to Mira, then Andi, and then touched my arm. "Because these three will kill all of them except who we decide to spare. Wetterick's people won't get one step closer to us than Jack wants, and even then, they're walking into a trap."

"Have we set traps?" Natif asked. He looked around with suspicion, since he was always in on any plans that involved fighting dirty. As a kid who grew up hard, it was his birthright to use whatever means necessary to win.

"No, and we're not going to. We *could* take them out with drones, but we're not going to do that either. I want something from them, and I can't get it from corpses," I said.

"Information?" Natif asked.

"No, I have all the information I need. Wetterick's people are opportunistic shits, and they have no place here. But we need hands to help as we grow, and we're going to need families and children and a second generation, and we can't secure that if I kill every one of them." I grinned at Natif, adding, "No matter how tempting that might be."

Silk raised her hands for silence at the buzz that rose in the crowd. "Andi and Jack found more sites to settle, and we need to start thinking about the future in terms of population, not just food. We have food. We have power, and more coming online each day. Soon enough, we're going to build our next city, and the next, and then we're going to be a state or a country. We need people to trust us, and to *want* to be here. They have skills, and we have everything else. It's time to do something other than just killing."

A murmur of agreement spread through the crowd. Silk was a born speaker, and I'd been right to choose her as my de facto second in command. Where Mira was cunning in the wild, Silk was cagey among civilization, or whatever passed for it now. Andi was good at everything, but as an engineer from my time, she had the same sense of dislocation that I had at times. We needed Andi to fix things, and build—not hold the hands of nervous settlers who just crossed ten days of desert wasteland.

Breslin raised an enormous hand. "Who goes with you to fight?"

"You do, among others," I told him. "We'll assign shooters. Mira will handle the sniping and take out anyone who looks competent. I suspect that Wetterick's people are bullies, not soldiers, but Mira will tag anyone who seems smarter than the rest."

"What's her range?" Breslin asked.

"That's classified," I said, earning a grin from Breslin.

Mira said nothing, a tight smile on her lips as she stared at Breslin without revealing anything.

He laughed, and bowed slightly to Mira. "I'm more of a smash-them-in-the-face guy, myself."

"And you'll have a chance to do just that. We're going to remove every target except the ones I need, and then we're going to bring them here for questioning," I said.

"Then what?" Breslin asked.

"Entirely up to them. I won't allow them to go free, just to warn The Outpost, but I'm not going to murder them in cold blood, either. Not unless they deserve it," I said.

"I can live with that," Breslin said.

"Good. We leave two hours before dawn. We

meet them at the wrecked wagons from the Harling's first trip. It gives us a shooting platform and clear vantage point, and we'll reduce them before they can even get organized," I said. "Let's get some sleep. If Mira picked you as a shooter, come with me. We need to explain some details about our deployment."

The meeting broke up in a flurry of low voices, but there was little to no outright worry except for a few mothers with small children. I understood their concern, and nodded to Silk, who moved into the crowd to reassure them that their children were going to be safe.

In five minutes, I had my snipers selected; two minutes after that I showed them where we would be positioned. The plan was brutal but simple, with few moving parts and maximum impact at long range. I also planned a surprise for the Outpost crew, because people who are willing to cross open desert to kill are rarely content to attack without some wrinkle in their plan. They might be simple brutes, but that didn't mean at least one of them wasn't cunning.

I spent a sleepless night on watch, strolling around the outside perimeter until Lasser met me under the crescent moon.

"Evening," he said, his voice coming out of the dark.

"Lasser. You should be resting." He was a tall, thin man with a nose like a hawk, but in the shadows, his face was all angles and planes except for his bright smile.

"No need. I find that as I age, I need less sleep. There's so much to do, and not enough sunlight to do it." I saw him give a rueful shake of his head. We had the strings of lights turned off to save the bulbs, because our reactor was barely working at all to provide us with juice.

"I don't need much either, but mine is mechanical, I think."

"What's it like?" he asked. "The—the 'bots?"

I considered the real question behind his inquiry, and gave him an honest answer, because he deserved it. "The short answer is—you'll find out soon enough. The long answer is I feel like I have the confidence of youth with the conscience of forty years. It's the best of both worlds, if you can manage it."

We were quiet as he digested my offer. "I would like to live much longer, if only to see Natif grow. I never had children of my own, not really. It was impossible to be a true parent under Wetterick."

"I plan on 'bots for whoever wants them. Within reason. I try to be fair, but long life and augmented abilities isn't for everyone. For one thing, I have no idea what it does to our ability to have children," I admitted.

"Andi would know," he said, astute as ever.

"She thinks she knows, but the nanobots we will be able to manufacture are several generations past most of her data. If we can find a library of some kind, we might be able to tap into advanced research, and move forward without the fear of rendering our best people sterile. In this land, that's a death sentence."

"Everything in this land is a death sentence," he said, and I found myself nodding along.

"How many are out there?" he asked after a moment.

"Could be as many as thirty, maybe more. Our rifles will take two dozen before they can break, and then we'll move in. I can move fast enough that they have no choice but to stand and fight. That's what I want," I said.

"Why?" Lasser's question was simple; honest.

"Because it isn't enough to win. We have to issue a decree. A law, sent from us to them. It's more than a fight. It's an invitation, and if I do it right, we gain up to a thousand people. If I do it wrong, I empower Wetterick to march on us in force, and then, I *do* have to kill everyone. That's the last thing I want, so it comes down to that youthful confidence and adult temper." I chuckled at the stupidity of reasoning about murder, but that was my world now. The Empty didn't care, and neither did many of the people in it.

"We'll have the center ready for your return," Lasser said, then looked to the stars. "About time to rally your troops. Two hours until dawn, if I mark it right."

He was right. I clasped his hand and slipped back into the homes, waking people with a quiet word. Many eyes were shining, having spent a sleepless night themselves. In ten minutes we were standing in a quiet column near the trucks. Andi drove one, and I drove the other, going slow and steady over the sketchy wagon path to intercept the raiders. When we had traveled for an hour, the sky was beginning to turn iron gray in the east, so we parked, stretched, and fanned out in our pre-planned array.

Mira checked her rifle, smiled, and slipped away like a wraith in the night. Andi sprawled in a shooter's position, and the other people were dark lumps along the ground, only their eyes and the gleam of rifle barrels giving their positions away.

I saw them before I heard them. They were stalking low, spread out and silent, heading southeast in a disciplined path. I counted thirty-eight raiders in all before taking cover behind a slumped cacti that had been struck by lightning in recent days. The charred barrel was wide enough to hide me, but low enough that I could see over it with ease.

When the raiders were a hundred meters out, I chirped the signal, and eight rifles barked in near unison, the reports rolling across the open desert like a curse from heaven. Seconds later, every rifle spoke again, and I began to see individual raiders dropping, arms flailing as the first scream reached our ears. I made the first casualties at six, then seven more, and then I fired, taking the head off a woman who was running toward us with an automatic weapon of her own. She spun back, lifeless, and then I fired again at a tall guy with spiked hair and a long gun.

My round took him in the thigh, sending him to the ground with a bellow of rage and pain. I saw several more raiders fall, and then their core of five leaders began to break left, trying to flank us in a move that made good sense.

Except for one tiny detail.

Mira's first round took one of the leaders in the chest, dropping him instantly. Before her report could fade, she fired again, taking a second raider in the neck that sprayed blood in a fountain, visible even to me as I raved to meet and refuse their flank.

Then my 'bot vision cleared and I saw what I wanted. Three men, well equipped, muscled, and clean, all moving with purpose despite losing two of their squad. These were the leaders—the elite— of Wetterick's forces.

At least the ones I hadn't killed.

They all raised weapons in smooth motions, but Mira fired again, killing the third man just as he got off a shot that split the skin of my ribs with a searing pain.

"Drop it, shitheads," I said, pulling a pistol as I drew up close enough to see the shock on their faces. Mira stood ten meters away, her rifle level and pointed at the head of the tallest man, who carried an undeniable command authority. Next to him was a short, stocky guy I recognized by sight if not name.

"Go fuck yours—"

Mira fired, and the short guy's head bloomed into a spray that dispersed like fog in the rising sun. The leader stood alone as two final shots rang out to our right. His people were gone. It was only him, and he tossed his rifle down with an expression of pure hatred.

"Name?" I asked, walking to him with my pistol drawing a bead on his nose.

"Glinn," he ground out.

"Jack Bowman. Start walking," I said, gesturing with my gun. "Do I have to say it?"

"Say what?" he asked, standing still.

"Fucking amateurs. I'll tell you the rules once. Walk, don't run. Don't speak. If you do anything I don't like, I'm not going to kill you," I said.

He raised a brow. He had a dark beard and eyes, with thick black hair. He could have been a general in another life, but now, he was a criminal.

"I won't kill you. I'll wound you—break both legs, slowly, most likely—and leave you here for the rattlers," I said.

"Or hogs. Or whatever those dinobird things are we're seeing," Mira said.

"Right. Anyway, you'll be coming out of the ass

of a creature inside a day, so walk, behave, and we'll have a chat at The Oasis. Now move."

He began to walk, holding himself well despite the hatred all my people directed his way. As an aside, I issued an order that made sense in The Empty. "Strip the bodies of gear. Leave them. Anything you find is yours. Kill any survivors."

"With pleasure, boss," came a voice, and my people moved off to the site of the slaughter. I heard a thin scream and the ripe splat of a machete, then nothing.

"Guess that's done," I told our guest.

When we reached the trucks, his brows went up again in disgust, and I knew he had no idea we were mobile. "We've got reactors, too. Hell, we saw you from the air when we did a recon pass."

"What the—" he started, then closed his mouth.

"Yep. Saw you, knew you were coming, and more importantly, I watched you burn that family with the wagons north of here. Not good, friend. That alone would get you good and dead, but not yet. We've got a lot to discuss," I said.

We rode in silence, watching him, and when we rolled up to The Oasis, a crowd came out to meet us.

"Get him to the chair," I said. He was bustled away by two burly men and Natif, who kept up a steady stream of curses that nearly made me blush. Silk met us with drinks and food, and I took ten minutes in our home to wash up and collect my thoughts.

Then I heard one of the Hannahs scream.

14

I BOLTED past Silk into the town center and came to a skidding stop.

Hannah was dragging Hannah Too away from our prisoner, holding her in a death grip around her small waist. Hannah was a spitting, sobbing ball of raw fury, unlike anything I'd ever seen in my life, and judging by the look on the raider's face, he knew Hannah.

It took several minutes to calm the uproar, punctuated by Lasser bringing out a bottle of whiskey and pouring a large cup for both Hannahs. They downed them like water, and Lasser refilled, then guided the girls to a seat where they proceeded to glare at the raider with a hatred I'd only seen in divorce court.

I held up my hands for silence, and after a moment, it was granted.

"What's your name?" I asked the raider.

To my surprise, he answered. "Taronic."

"Hannah, you know him?" I asked. Both Hannahs—one blonde, one brunette, and both filled with righteous fury—nodded.

Hannah Too spoke first. "This piece of shit killed Milya last year. Raped her so bad she bled out and he didn't even stay. Snuck out and said he was never in the house. Wetterick protected him, so we couldn't do anything about it." She spat at him, falling far short but making her point.

"Raped?" I asked, my voice going dangerously soft. I could feel my fingers begin to twitch as I fought the urge to kill Taronic without a single question.

"She was a whore," he said, his voice flat.

I nodded, looking down. "She was. And a girl, I assume?"

"Seventeen," Hannah answered.

"Seventeen," I repeated, as if the word was a shit sandwich. I shrugged, leaning close to Taronic, who was tied to the chair with thick wire. He wasn't going anywhere, but my rage would have to wait a moment. "Do you trust me, Hannah? And Hannah? Silk? All of you?"

I got a chorus of agreement, and Silk came over to touch my arm.

She whispered, "Make sure this doesn't cost you too much."

"Okay," I said, and she stepped away, fixing Taronic with a sad smile.

"Wetterick. I need to know his strength," I said.

Taronic looked around, finding no one in his corner. "Two hundred guns, give or take, depending on sickness or injury. We've been training hard for this ever since we found the hospital."

"Hospital? Where?" I asked.

"East of us. Some bonecutter from Kassos came out, said he was looking for a lab, whatever that is. He went on for hours about viral loads and cracking retrovirus or—something. I couldn't understand it. None of us could, really, but he convinced everyone that he could build weapons to kill off the wild tribes out east. Probably you, too, once he found out about this place. Like I said, we were training for a lot of other things, so I wasn't paying too much attention to some asshole with medical equipment," Taronic said.

"What other things?" I asked. Andi came close, watching him with unblinking eyes.

"Going west. And south. *We* heard about you, of course, and others, but you were first on our list. We—knew things," he said, his eyes cutting away.

"What things?" I asked him, feeling a chill in my gut.

"The reactors. The Cache. Other things." Taronic looked into the crowd, then his head snapped back to face me.

In the direction he'd glanced stood Danto, looming in front of Breslin's family. Danto wore a sour expression, his glower just short of open rebellion.

"And how soon will the whole force move on us?" I asked.

"Won't," Taronic admitted. "We're going to the Cache. This place is small coin compared to all that."

"True. We won't be, not for long, but it's not a bad move." I nodded, considering his words, then I stepped back and lifted my voice so everyone could hear. "I told you I would never be a tyrant, and I won't. I told you I'd keep you safe. I will. But there are things you can't know right now that can hurt us, and as strong as we are, we can't afford a standup fight with hundreds of soldiers. Not if we want to grow, and have kids, and live in peace."

I moved to stand next to Taronic, my hand on his shoulder. I held no weapon, and my face was blank. "It isn't just that he raped and killed a girl, though that would be bad enough. It isn't his actions in The Empty, when he burned that family and ended their lives. His crimes are far worse than that, because he has a secret, and even now, he can't bring himself to tell the truth. Can you?"

"I don't know what you're—" Taronic began, and I tore his throat out with my fingers. I dropped the section of windpipe to the ground as he sput-tered and gasped, a river of blood streaming down the front of his leather armor.

No one spoke save some children, who began to cry. I wiped my hand on his armor, and then twisted his head nearly off, the bones breaking with dull thumps.

And then I walked toward Danto, who shrank back in horror, his faced gone dead white.

I put out a hand and moved him aside. "Why did you do it?" I asked Jossi, who stood behind him and next to a stunned Breslin. "Why are you a spy?"

15

Jossi had the good sense—or arrogance—not to say a word of denial. People moved away from her like she carried the plague, and in seconds, there was a ring of empty space with only Jossi, Breslin, and me.

"Jossi?" Breslin asked, disbelief in his voice.

When she finally looked up at him, her blue eyes were narrowed, lips twisted in a sneer that transformed her completely. Breslin took an involuntary step back, and I wanted to, though I held firm in case she was armed.

Then she spoke to me.

"You can't imagine what it's like, having this beast come at you in bed. Pawing me, lying beside me, reeking of dirt and sweat."

Breslin deflated in horror as his wife became something else—*someone* else with each word that fell out of her lips. Their children stood in mute horror next to Natif, unsure what to say. They were old enough to understand, but what she was saying was beyond comprehension.

"Beast?" I asked her. "This man? He works harder than anyone here."

Jossi flicked a glance at the Hannahs, then laughed, and the noise was like a knife. "You think you're whores, but you don't know what it's like to give up everything to raise children in a stinking shithole of a camp, when I could have been a council daughter. I would have had—everything. Clothes. A staff to care for me instead of fending for a family who thought that success was finding two meals in a row."

Beba walked briskly across the gravel and slapped Jossi across the mouth, hard. "I always knew you thought you should have a crown, but to do this to your own children? Don't insult the Hannahs. You're no whore. A whore has *goals*. You have a fantasy."

Jossi laughed again. "Better than living like—"

Beba's hand cracked across Jossi's face for the

second time. "Not one more word." She turned to address me, and the calm healer was still there, but just barely. Beba was a woman transformed, too. She was a mother, protecting her son and his children, and when she spoke, it was in a voice so devoid of emotion I felt a chill on my arms. "Will you kill her for spying? It's obvious she did it to secure a place in Kassos."

"A place?" Jossi asked through bloody teeth. Her children were crying now. Breslin stood mute. Mira, Silk, and Andi looked like they wanted to shoot Jossi on the spot, but the angriest face was Derin, who had walked up just in time to see the spectacle. He had a protective arm around Scoot, who leaned against him instinctively. "A palace. Not a *place*. Everything I deserved. Everything I *earned*."

"Earned? By what?" Beba asked. "Being born pretty? You haven't earned anything, except the love of your children, and you just threw that away. You sicken me."

"How did you do it?" I asked Jossi.

"I waited until he was sleeping, and took a message outside the perimeter. They picked it up. They've known about this place since we arrived," she said without a hint of regret.

"You got a lot of people killed for your chance at a paper crown," I said. "Not that you care."

"I don't," Jossi said, defiant.

I addressed Breslin and Beba as one, lifting my voice so it could be heard. A hum of stunned shock hung over the area, and my next words had to be carefully chosen. Taronic's corpse still hung from his final place not ten meters away. I had killed to protect The Oasis, and now, I had to do something different to assure the same outcome.

"I won't touch her, and I won't allow anyone else to either," I said, shooting a glance toward the Hannahs, who stared at Jossi with fevered intensity. "This should be a family decision, but we're past that now. She's a spy, and she put us all at risk. She brought Taronic south, and cost a family their lives. They died badly." I fought the urge to spit, reminded of the scene we saw from the air, with burning bodies and shattered wagons.

"You wanted . . . a crown?" Breslin asked his wife.

Her sneer faded, replaced by something even worse. Pity.

"Like you would understand. I was turned out from the city and left to my own devices because of —politics. And then you came along and I couldn't go back to Kassos because I would have been killed. It's a snake pit of lies, and I was outside looking in. So I let you climb on me and fill my belly with children, each one wearing me out and making me more like the women who trudge to the fountains in Kassos for water each day." She shook her head with regret, and her lack of caring was so perfect she might have been made of clay.

Breslin said nothing, but he stepped back and gathered his children in his arms, muttering quiet assurance. Beba did the same, and it was only me and Jossi in the space. She was alone, and she was hated.

But I wouldn't kill her.

"Danto," I said.

"Yes?" he asked in surprise.

"Do you want to be here or not?" I asked him.

"I do."

"Then I have a job for you. Silk and Mira will get packs together. Take Jossi north," I said.

"I told you I can't go back to Kassos, idiot!" Jossi snapped.

"Kassos? Who said anything about Kassos? You're going to the site where those traders were killed. Danto is going to watch you bury their bodies, one at a time. You're going to give them a decent burial with your own hands, princess, and then he's going to march you back here where you'll be given a choice," I said.

"What? Are you out of your fucking mind? I'm not going into the—"

"I wasn't done. You're coming back here, and you'll open a stall doing paper work, making dyes —things you're good at. Breslin will keep his children. You've lost that privilege, but I will not kill you. That decision lies somewhere else," I said.

My words sank in, and Jossi stared, dumbstruck by the knowledge that someone other than me held her fate. "Who?"

"Your children. When they come of age, they decide if you stay or are exiled. It's up to them, not me, and not anyone else. *Your* children, who you threw away over a chance at something shiny," I said. The words felt like rot on my tongue, but I said them anyway.

Jossi was pale, swaying on her feet. Danto came up, his eyes on her with a wary distrust. "What if she runs?"

"She won't. She's a coward," I said.

Danto led her away, and for the first time since I'd woken in that tube, I felt the true meaning of sadness.

16

It took a full day for The Oasis to return to some kind of normal.

I dragged Taronic's body into the desert and left if for scavengers, because he didn't deserve the effort it would have taken to bury him. He made a choice, and even in death, he would live with it.

Breslin clung to his children, and Beba kept them with her as she began to build a clinic in earnest. She was training the kids to be healers, whether they knew it or not, and it made a kind of sense that families should pass skills on without concern for things like school. The Empty was our school, and it was a hard one. We were carving out a place to live, one sapling at a time, but in the meantime, learning took place every day through the work we did.

I chose to lead by example, digging and planting thirty saplings along the newest channel, just past the eastern pond that Breslin and Lasser had completed. It would be a place for fish, we decided, so Mira took Natif and some of the other kids to a small creek about ten klicks west of us. It was the first significant water we'd seen on our way to The Oasis, and it had pools deep enough to hold fish.

After four hours, they came back, a chattering mass of excitement led by Natif. Each kid carried a small bucket filled with fish.

Mira was grinning at the excited mass of kids. "The fish never stood a chance."

"What did they find?" I asked, looking in each bucket. Dark shapes swam, most of them small but a few large enough that I could tell they would be big fish in a few months. There were catfish, crappie, sandbass, and largemouth, all alive and well.

"Dump 'em in and see what happens. Let's keep the catfish in the western pond, and everything else goes east. Sound good?" I asked the kids. Their shout of agreement was followed by a mass charge as they split up in two directions, sloshing water and shrieking as they pelted over the gravel paths.

Mira sighed. "That was harder than scavenging. They wouldn't . . . stop . . . talking."

I draped an arm over her shoulders, laughing at the frustration in her voice. "Kids are like that, especially when they're excited."

"I think I'll have Lasser do that next time," she said.

"Can't. While you were away, I made an official declaration. You're in charge of all youth activities. It's a fulltime job, so you'll have to—"

"Tell Silk and Andi that we've suddenly developed lockjaw?" she said, raising a threatening brow.

"Well, as long as your *knees* aren't locked, I could survive for a bit, I guess."

She leaned in to nip my ear, then pushed me away and went to wash up. It was time for lunch, and people were starting to come in from their various projects, tired and dirty. They were talking —not as much as two days ago, but still, it was something close to normal, and that would have to do for the time being until we learned how to process Jossi's betrayal. I still wasn't entirely sure what it meant, and that was part of my job.

I took a seat after scrubbing myself clean in the sink, my black hair dripping as I filled drink cups for the line of people forming, and by the time I had my food, I was dry and thinking of the jobs that faced me for the rest of the day.

Andi slid next to me, her eyes glittering with excitement. "Get the girls. And Lasser. Our house in one minute." She walked away, mumbling to herself, and I felt another chill of uncertainty on my neck, but this time it was the sensation of something bigger than a raiding party.

We were in the main room of our house, excited and uncertain as Andi thumbed her tablet to life then tilted it toward the wall. "Close the door," she said.

Lasser pushed the door closed, and it was darker. An image flared to life on the wall, and I knew what I was seeing. "Drone footage?" I asked. Andi's tablet was projecting the raw feed from the Condor at a massive height. Far below, our Vampires were visible as bland triangles on the wind. Their camouflage worked at every angle, and I knew we would be able to use them in a variety of future missions.

"I can barely see the ground," Mira said. Silk made a noise of agreement, so Andi touched her tablet. The picture began to zoom, first straight down, and then in wide, sweeping arcs as the camera lens began to employ a specific search pattern.

"When we were at our farthest northeast, I had the drone look toward a line of trees. It's a river, and I'm not sure what it is because it wasn't there when I was working in the area. You can see from the drone that it's far more than just a tree line," Andi said.

"It's a forest. Like ours, but bigger. Older. Things look green," Mira said.

"There's grass, too," Lasser added, and his tone told me he hadn't seen grass in a long time. The Empty was changing, and quickly. Part of it was due to our efforts, but other changes were happening that I couldn't explain.

"Among other things," Andi said cryptically. "Look here." She pointed to a dry creek bed, glinting in the harsh sunlight.

"A dry channel. So what?" Mira asked. There were thousands of them across the desert, and other than turning into raging torrents during storms, they had no use but as game trails.

"Not a dry bed. I noticed something when I was looking at the footage. It's too big to be creek rock. It's excavated. Tailings from a mine, if I'm guessing, and recent. That means there's an active mining operation going on less than a hundred klicks from here, and I couldn't figure out who would be doing it because there was no sign of houses. No tents, no buildings, and not even any tracks. If there are people working a mine, then they would be trading. There's no evidence of that here," Andi said.

I watched her for a moment, then smiled. "But you found something else."

"Fucking right I did. Do you believe in fairy tales? Because I do now," she said.

She drew the view down, magnifying as the camera focused on a small clearing about forty meters inside the tree line. There was a large, flat stone and a shape in front of it. It was pale, nearly luminous in the dappled light of the tree cover, and only visible when the drone had been banking hard while the camera was running.

"Magnify further?" I said, my voice just above a whisper. I thought I knew what I was seeing, but I didn't dare believe it.

"Going closer," Andi said, and the pixelated view lost focus, then cleared to reveal a pale woman with skin like a statue. She was alabaster white, thin, and wore goggles that held her blonde hair back from a long neck. She was smiling, and in her hand she held a rifle of inhuman design, more art than weapon. As the video ran on, she smiled up at the Condor one last time, turned, and lifted the door masked as a rock, then descended down steps into perfect darkness.

The Condor lost sight of her, and the clearing, and then it flew away from the forest heading west.

"Holy shit," Mira breathed.

"Was she human?" Lasser asked.

Andi nodded, and I did too.

"There was this story from before I was born. A book called *The Time Machine*. There were people in it who lived underground, and they were pale like that, but I always expected them to be short, for some reason. She wasn't," I said.

"Morlocks. They ate people," Andi said grimly.

"In the book they did. As to her, I have no idea, but did you see that rifle?" I asked, bewildered by the design.

"Think about it," Andi said. "Two thousand years underground? Their own culture growing in a world that's ripped apart by the virus? I'm surprised she didn't have—hell, I don't know, wings or something. And we're not even considering the real issue here. The location of that forest, and wherever she went underground."

"The Eden Chain," I said.

"The very same. It's in the right location, and it had enormous resources to see people through the end of the world. I don't think they just survived, I think they adapted, or even self-selected and engaged in gene design," Andi said,

"What does that mean?" Silk asked. She was brilliant, but she needed context to grasp what we meant.

"They bred themselves to life underground, and now they look different than we do, even though they're still human. There's only so much you can do with people," Andi said.

"Not true," I told her. "Ogres."

"Shit, you're right. That means they found a way to change without reverting, maybe. We don't know if they succeeded right away, or if they made an army of flawed beings on their way to what we saw. Only one way to find out," Andi said.

"Go and ask them," Mira said.

"Go and ask," I agreed.

"I'm going to go tell everyone, and reassure them that nothing will happen while we're away," I said, rising, but Silk put her hand on my arm.

"I'll stay. Lasser will stay. Take Andi and Breslin, leave Lasser, Beba, Derin, and me here. We'll keep control and move forward with projects. Lasser can continue the channels, we'll plant the next rows of trees, and I can run wire for the new street. We have plenty of rifles and command on tap. I'll see to it," Silk said.

I gave her suggestion consideration. She was right, because Andi was the engineer, and I had a suspicion we would need her when we met the people who lived hidden away from the sun.

"Okay. It's in your hands," I said.

She leaned up on tiptoes to kiss me. "I'll bring a go-bag to the trucks. You should leave now, I think."

"Same here. Whatever Wetterick will do, Kassos will follow, and we need to contact those people before anyone else. We need allies, and they don't know it yet, but they need us," I told her.

"Why?" Silk asked, her brow furrowed lightly.

"Because Andi and I are the only link between their world and this one, and I hope they see that survival depends on both parts of that equation."

17

Andi rode up front, with Breslin in the back, brooding but alert. He held a rifle in his hands, making it look like a toy. It had been a challenge to convince him to go, but when he saw the footage, he understood that mine and Andi's presence was just the hint of something bigger. With his mind open to the possibility of a stable place for his children, he said a tearful goodbye and left them in Beba's capable hands. By the time we were rolling east, his kids were running with Natif, and I heard the big man sigh in his first deep breath of two days.

I looked at Andi, who watched him and then shrugged. No one knew how people dealt with the pain of betrayal, but I had my suspicion that

Breslin was made of tough stuff, and after a few hours on the desert, he would find his focus.

I was right.

After our first break to check the truck and eat, he came up to me, blocking the sun while I checked a tire.

"Thank you," he said, then walked away to stare at a snake that watched us from a small pile of rock.

"Progress," Andi said. "We're good. Cells are running cool, and we've got plenty of water. Onward."

"Onward it is, then," I agreed.

We would avoid going all the way to the Cache, and break north and then east to pick up bits of available road when we could. There were two massive washouts in our path, but the truck was high enough that we could drive through any creek at the bottom, provided the fords we saw from the air hadn't collapsed. The stream banks were wildly unpredictable, and I learned to expect the worst out here in The Empty.

"First ford should be just—there," Andi said after another thirty minutes. We had two solid hours of daylight left, and I wanted to get across the first obstacle before pulling up for the night. As I drove forward, I didn't see the bank.

Instead, I saw a flurry of wings.

"Blood chickens? On something big?" I asked myself, then Andi found the range with her sight as well. "Huge, whatever it is."

"That rhino you saw? Long way from the driftwood jumble," she said.

"What's that?" Breslin asked, peering forward.

"Scavengers on something big, and a lot of them. More than I've ever seen in one place," I said with a wary note. As a rule, dead things were bad, because they attracted things that liked to kill.

"Go on foot?" Andi asked, but I shook my head. I didn't care about the squabbling horde of blood chickens. I cared about being mobile enough to leave in a hurry. Just in case. The idea that something brought down an animal big enough to cast a shadow made me wary of being unprotected, no matter how badass my 'bots thought I could be.

"Gun ready, Breslin." Andi had her rifle out the window, sighted and ready as we edged closer. I could hear the complaining mass of scavengers even two hundred meters away, their wings beating at each other and the ground to cause a dust cloud that rose twenty meters before dispersing.

"Jack, how big was that rhino you saw?" Andi asked, her voice low and filled with awe.

"Huge. Tons. Bigger than anything I've ever seen before," I told her, peering through the chaos of blood chickens and their endless brawl for food.

"Is that thing . . . bigger?" she asked.

Breslin was staring too, his mouth open as we came close enough to send some of the birds skyward in a torrent of squawking anger.

"Not just bigger. Taller, too," I said. "I'm getting out. Cover me."

I left the truck, took a good look around, and started moving toward the carcass with slow, deliberate steps. The stench was eyewatering, like a physical blow that filled my nose and mouth. I spat and cleared my mouth, but the stink returned, more powerful than ever. I got within five meters of the beast and began to understand what I was looking at.

Rather, I tried to make sense of it. My mind rejected the sheer scale of the creature, but there it was, in glorious, stinking death right before me.

Andi called to me from the truck, waving her tablet. "You're not going to believe this."

"What is it?" I asked, staring at the enormous body. The chest and body cavity were nearly empty, but the rest of the animal was intact. It was covered in tough gray hide with speckles near the shoulders, a long, thick neck, and legs that were half again longer than me. Standing, it would have been seven meters tall, easily, and it had to weigh twenty tons. There was no way this animal should be here, not even in a world gone mad with a virus that could make people into ogres.

Andi was out of the truck, Breslin standing next to her with his eyes flicking nervously across the scene. She held up her tablet, and a drawing of the dead animal was on screen.

"Indricothere?" I asked. "I'm not entirely up on my megafauna, but didn't they die out a couple million years ago or something?"

"More like fifteen million years, at least." She pulled at her lip, thinking.

"What is it?" I asked.

"Before I went in the tube, more than one team was bringing the mammoth back. Let's say it worked, and I have no reason to doubt it because they had run trials with smaller animals, like extinct seals. This," she said with a wave at the beast, "would be just the kind of thing some idiot would try, and there was a good amount of time between my nap and the end of the world."

"Which means we have no idea what's out here, and overseas," I said.

"And *under* the seas. I'm not saying they brought all kinds of animals back, but if we don't understand the virus, and we don't know how it went haywire," she wondered.

"This thing was natural? At some point?" Breslin asked.

"Completely. The planet was covered with giant animals like this for tens of millions of years, and for a hundred million before that, but those were different. Dinosaurs, amphibians, giant bugs. Your basic nightmare," Andi said.

I walked closer to the creature, touching the skin. It felt like an elephant, but the scale was mind-boggling. Then I heard a low *whuff*, and I pulled a blade, whirling to my right with all the speed and power my singing blood would allow.

The giant cat burst from cover behind a shrub so small it wouldn't cast a shadow at noon. His face was smeared in gore, giant fangs bared and paws flaring into circles tipped with claws as long as my hand. The hide was a flawless match for the dull grasses around us, and the cat hit me like a comet as I drove my knife up into its neck, steel bursting through the hide with a sickening *pop*. I rolled my hip, letting the creature's enormous weight carry it past me to crash into the dead Indricothere with a resounding thud.

The entire fight lasted less time than a cowboy would stay on a steer.

I wiped blood from eyes and stood on shaky legs, letting my blade drop to the ground. After two calming breaths, I turned to Andi and Breslin, who both looked at me with eyes gone round from horror. To her credit, Andi's gun was up and ready, but Breslin was frozen.

"You okay?" I asked as casually as I could with my heart threatening to break my ribs.

"What . . . the . . . *fuck*," Breslin breathed.

"I kinda feel the same way. Eyes up, Andi. Those cats don't hunt alone." I found my rifle—which I'd dropped in the attack—checked it, and began sweeping the area. I wouldn't trust anything bigger than a loaf of bread, because it could hide one of the giant cats. When we made a circuit of the kill, I told Andi and Breslin to stand guard while I pulled my smaller knife.

"What are you doing, Jack?" Andi asked, watching me kneel beside the cat. It wasn't a liger. It was too big, at least eight hundred kilos or more. The mane was small, the ears tight to the head, and the body thick and powerful. The paws were something to behold, being twice the size of a dinner plate.

"I want a souvenir. Sort of." I slipped the blade into the dead cat and began skinning in quick, decisive motions.

"Why?" Breslin asked.

I looked up through eyes that stung from sweat. The cat's innards were steaming hot. I grunted as I worked, pausing to answer his question. "Because I might not ever see another one of these, and I want to remember this day. I would never kill for fun, but I'll be damned if I leave this here to the blood chickens and worms. This is my fucking kill, and it's going home with us."

"Okay," Andi agreed, but she held up a hand of warning. "If you think we're making love on a lionskin rug, you're out of your mind. I'm not joining you for your weird 1970s porn cosplay. You feel me?"

I laughed, turning the cat over to finish cutting. "Loud and clear. No rughumping."

"Rughumping? What's wrong with you people? That thing just tried to *eat* him," Breslin said, stunned.

"Yeah, but I got the drop on him, and now we

can use him. He's just a predator, Breslin. He was doing what he was made for, and I answered him by doing what *I'm* made for now. Nothing personal. Just business," I said. "You see?"

Breslin got my point, even if my casual attitude about death at the jaws of a giant cat made him uneasy. "I guess I do, Jack."

"Good man. Now use those muscles and help me flip this bastard again. I want to get gone before his family comes looking for dad," I said.

In fifteen minutes, the hide was off, and I had to think about how to preserve it until we returned. "When we set up camp, we need to be near water. I'll wash the hide and stretch it over the truck."

"Going to draw predators, Jack," Breslin said.

"We're taking watches anyway, so I like our chances. Then, we keep an eye out for salt. Rock salt is best, but just drying the hide will give us a chance to get it home. We could piss on it, but even I'm not ready to go that far," I said.

"What?" Andi asked. "Urine? *Human* urine?"

"Yeah, sure. It's got ammonia in it. Haven't you ever watched those prepper shows, or—never mind. You were an engineer. You probably thought prepping was a waste of time," I said, nudging her with my elbow.

She pulled away, flicking her fingers in distaste at my general state of bloody disrepair. "Number one, wash up before you touch me, you brute, and two—I preferred vintage cartoons, when I watched TV at all," she said with an air of dignity.

"I respect you even more, woman," I told her, hefting the hide on top of the truck.

I washed up and we left the site, watching the shrieking blood chickens return before we had even pulled away.

"Jack, I have a question," Breslin said.

"Sure, fire away," I answered, never taking my eyes off the ground ahead.

"What the hell is TV?"

18

SLEEP DID NOT COME EASY, but not for a bad reason. Instead, we were taken in by the meteor shower that set the sky in motion, peaking just before dawn with an array of luminous streaks that made afterimages in my eyesight.

"I've never seen anything like that," I said, and even I could hear the wonder in my voice. There had been dozens of meteors per hour for the length of my watch, and I'd woken Andi to watch it with me. Breslin got up on his own, and together, we spent an hour watching the incandescent lines carve up the sky as each meteor burned into nothing.

"I never saw the stars at all," Andi said. "More of a city girl."

"I was a suburbs kid, but my grandparents farmed. We would see meteor showers in the summer now and then. This is different," I said, then tore my eyes away from the sky, seeing the first light of day pushing at the eastern horizon.

"I think the whole world is different, Jack." Andi sounded like she was just beginning to accept our reality. I could relate. There were moments that jarred me, like seeing the giant animals, or an ogre, or even people carrying swords and pistols because the land would chew them up if they didn't defend themselves.

We broke camp quietly, driving as the day grew bright. I was just cresting a low hill when I saw a wagon. Then I saw another, and then a third, all in a line and pulled by something that looked rather like oxen.

"Traders? Out here?" Andi asked.

"There's not much trade this way," Breslin added. "At least not if they want to live. East to west, yes, but not north by south. The paths aren't good enough for anything permanent."

"Let's ask them," I said.

I drove slowly, lights on and approaching at a slight angle. The people saw us, pulled weapons, and fell back in a smooth motion. They were organized and calm, pulling the children into the center wagon while men and women stood in a loose perimeter. I saw guns, a longbow, and a tall woman who held what had to be a crossbow. All in all, they looked well-fed and capable.

Just the kind of people I was hoping to find.

"Guns ready, but I think these are people we want to meet," I said, leaving the truck in park. "Andi, driver's seat. Breslin, alongside the passenger door, and weapons ready but not aimed, if you please. No need to spook them."

"Got it," Andi said, sliding over without taking her eyes off the people.

I made a show of slipping my rifle over my back, waving, and stepping carefully toward the wagons. The lead knot of people—two men and a woman—stepped forward, not hiding their guns but not pointing them at me, either. So far, so good.

"Hallooo," I called, waving again.

The short man waved, a cautious smile on his face. He was powerfully built, dark, and wore a wide-brimmed hat with a band of lizard skin around it. To his left stood a woman who could be his sister, and to his right, a tall, skinny guy with a face like a rat and eyes that never blinked.

I walked slowly, with purpose, and drew up ten meters away. "Are you traders?" I asked.

"Maybe," the center man answered.

"Got any salt?" I asked.

He cut his eyes at his companions, then looked back to me. "Maybe."

"I'm going to go back to my truck and get something to show you. If you can help us, great. If not, we'll be on our way, and wish you well. It's not a weapon. I'm going to carry it back here, slowly. Sound fair?" I said.

"Not one twitch," the tall guy hissed.

"Shut up, Monte," the leader said without looking at him. "Go ahead. We'll wait."

I walked back to the truck, my back itching from their eyes, smiled at Andi, and grabbed the hide. I carried it back like it was a bomb, placed it on the ground in front of me, and unrolled it, all under the gaze of dozens of people.

"If you have salt, we'll trade or buy it. I'd like to save this, I think," I said.

"What is that?" the leader asked.

"Giant cat of some kind. It was eating a kill about twenty klicks back. Tried to make me the second part of the meal, but I took issue with that," I said.

The man walked toward me, then used a boot to unroll the hide some more. "You're saying you killed this thing?"

"That's exactly what I'm saying."

He stared at me, saw I was serious, then noticed the puncture in the hide. His eyes flicked to the swords on my back, and he whistled softly. "Monte, ask Doc to bring his gear up here. You washed the hide?" he asked me.

"Right after the kill. Dry now," I said.

He grinned, and it was the first natural expression on his face. "We have a little experience saving skins, but nothing like this. You say it was south of here?"

"It was, and the carcass it was eating was the biggest animal I've ever seen. I know what it is, but it's not supposed to be here," I said.

He took his hat off, wiping his face with a broad hand, then put the hat back with a decisive tug. "Have your people come over for a drink. We should probably talk."

"What's your name?" I asked.

He put his hand out. It was thick with callous and muscle. A working hand. "Stanger. My people are a mix of family and friends. We've been trading for nearly twenty years since our wells ran dry up north."

"Jack Bowman, and I'm the lead of a settlement just south of here. We've water if you need it," I said.

"Might take you up on that depending on our chat. You like whiskey?" he asked me.

"No, I don't. I love whiskey."

He thumped my back, laughing. "I think we're gonna get along just fine, Jack."

After our introductions, Stanger's people took the cat hide and began rubbing coarse salt into it with small brushes. They worked quickly, wasting no motion and turning the hide so that each section was treated three times.

"They know what they're doing," I remarked as we sat on boxes in the shade of an extendable awning. We had cool water and a flask of whiskey that was young, but not too rough. I took a sip, handed it to Andi, and then waited for Stanger to speak. Breslin leaned against the wagon, casting a shadow all his own, but he was smiling because there were kids around and they seemed to gravitate to the big man.

"You're from the south?" Stanger asked.

I'd already gotten a subtle nod from Andi, who

knew what I was going to discuss. "We are. The Free Oasis, to be exact. We're growing, we have the rule of law, and I have plans."

"What kind of plans?" he asked. His other people were listening intently as well.

"Short version? I'm going to rebuild a working state, water systems, technology, power grid, dams, and roads. We're going to have all the trappings of civilization without any of the bullshit you see in Kassos or Wetterick's place."

Stanger looked openly dubious. "That's quite a goal."

"I agree, which is why we're so busy," I replied, folding my hands and waiting for him to continue.

He only hesitated for a minute, but it was enough. This was a man in trouble, despite his assured outward appearance. He had around eighty people by my count, and they were on the move for a reason, not just trade.

"The salt is yours. Do you charge for safe passage through your lands?" Stanger asked.

"No, and they're not my lands. They belong to everyone for now. As The Oasis expands, our law will become the dominant structure, along with our actual buildings. Wherever we find water, we build. Where we build, we plant trees, and we're going to reclaim The Empty, one community at a time," I said.

"And what of Wetterick?" he asked on a neutral tone.

I held out my hand, regarding it with mild interest. "See this hand? I used to kill Taronic less than two days ago. You know him?"

"I—yes. I did, anyway. Mean bastard," Stanger said.

"Not anymore. We took out an entire raiding party and saved him for last. He killed a girl, and two of my citizens knew him. The choice was his, and he made it some time ago. I say that the rule of law will hold control over this area, but I have limits. Slavery is out. Keeping ogres is out. Rape, theft, and other crimes like that are all out. We're going to have a free society, but it will also be based on personal responsibility. If you can't care for yourself, and you harm others?" I flexed my hand, and Stanger nodded. We had an understanding.

"May I ask where you're going now?" He looked at our truck, and his brows lifted with more than simple curiosity. He clearly knew what the vehicle was, but it wasn't commonplace in this world.

"Northeast, and that's all I can say for now, but

I have a proposition for you based on how you answer a question. An offer, if you will, for you and your people," I said.

"I'm listening."

"Why are you on the move?" I asked.

"It's not safe on our range anymore," he answered without hesitation.

"Why?" I leaned forward, sensing he was telling an uncomfortable truth.

"Among other things, raiders, and not the kind who just want cattle. We've lost people to them in attacks, and they've stolen women, children, even a few young boys. Then there are the beasts," he said.

"What kind? I thought you would be used to almost anything, being out here in The Empty," I told him.

"I was. And then monsters started showing up. Things I can't even describe, and big—big as a house, some of them. Horns, hooves, teeth. All of them hard to bring down and wherever they went came things chasing them. Like that cat you killed, which was a damn fine piece of work, if you don't mind me saying so." His tone was envious. He was a man who knew how easy it was to die out here.

"I killed it on a carcass that was—well, show him, Andi?"

She brought her tablet out and pulled up an image of the Indricothere. Eyebrows went up all around at the exotic tech, but the picture elicited a comment from nearly every member of Stanger's party. "I take it you've seen one of these?"

"Sure did. Thorneaters, we call them. Not often, but new in the past year or so, like they're being driven. Or born, though I have no idea how something that big could be anything less than a hundred years old," Stanger said. "Is that— computer there—an indicator of how you're running things?"

"It is. We're reclaiming the old world, before the virus. The good parts, anyway," I said.

"I think I would like that," Stanger said, and just then, he sounded tired.

"If you don't mind, I'd like to meet your people, Stanger, and I'd like them to see us as well, because I don't know a lot about cattle, but I have an idea," I said. As we talked, I took note of the condition of his people, their wagons, and the absence of any other commanders. I let my eyes play over the horizon, finding what I was looking for then pulling my attention back to the people around me. My moment of thought was broken by the distinct crow of a rooster, and Stanger jerked his thumb toward a wagon that had cages. "Chickens, too. We have a portable oven for baking."

"Chickens and cattle," Andi said. "Those sound like the good parts of life, don't they?" She smiled at me, and I knew she understood my thoughts.

"They sure do," I agreed. We stood as Stanger began to introduce us, walking from wagon to wagon, shaking hands and murmuring words of greeting. Some of the looks we got were guarded, some friendly, but none were hostile. The people were tough, hard-working, and self-reliant, just as I had hoped. When we finished our circuit, the cook wagon was beginning a meal, and Stanger invited us to stay. I accepted and asked him to walk with us for a minute.

"I know you have responsibilities, so I won't waste your time. If you would like to join us at The Oasis, you're welcome to go right now," I said.

He drew up, regarding me with his dark eyes in a moment of intense scrutiny. "All of us?"

"Yes. Every last one, even the old aunties who are fussing over the chickens," I said.

"Especially them," Andi added.

Stanger smiled, then wiped his face again with a cloth. He was buying time to think, and I let him because it was a big decision. "My people are self-sufficient, but that won't last. What can you offer us? You see what we have, and while it isn't much, it's something. We have skilled labor, too, across a lot of different crafts, but none of us use Hightec like you do, even though I work and trade with it. Hightec makes a lot of money, but it's inconsistent."

"I'm more interested in saving what you have," I said.

"Saving?" he asked, mild confusion on his face.

"You've led them across The Empty, and you're doing a damned fine job of it, but eventually, you'll start to lose people. You know how this place is. It might be a fall into a washout, or a predator, or some rogue band of raiders, but you'll lose people the longer you're out here. That won't happen at The Oasis, and you'll have homes, water, food, and a place to earn a living in safety. You have my word."

"And mine," Andi said.

"Mine too," Breslin said with a decisive nod. "Jack took my family in when we had nowhere to go. My children are safe as we speak. My mother is a doctor, and I sleep in a bed at night, not under the stars wondering if the wild things are going to take my family in the night. It's a good place."

Stanger took Breslin's words to heart, because he saw something in him that he recognized. The big man was a fellow parent and survivor on the way to something better, and not entirely sure if he could keep his family safe on the way. Their shared reality had far more impact than my invitation, and I saw Stanger make his mind up that instant.

"The cattle need water, and a lot of it. They browse on almost anything but feeding them is a constant challenge. The chickens are simple, and they breed easily. The cattle need a fence, but the chickens stay close to their coop, and they're damned useful at getting rid of pests," Stanger said.

"We have water and land in abundance. What we don't have is people. I can tell you we have no need of your animals for food. We hunt, and we have means of extending our hunting range a huge distance. You would have at least a year or more before we even think about changing that policy," I said, and he nodded, looking relieved that I didn't see his herd as a walking cheeseburger stand. "Our policy is simple. You're given help and materials, and you build your home. We have two hundred people and we're growing, and the command structure is small. Your people, your rules—as long as they don't engage in crimes against others, but I get the feeling that's discouraged." I smiled because I knew a clean operation when I saw it, and Stanger's people had the look of a community that understood their survival depended on each other. "We have areas where we're building craft stalls, too. Those are free. We have no taxes, and no money, and we'll stay that way as long as we can."

"Do the craft stalls have access to water?" he asked.

"They do. What do you have in mind?" I asked.

"We have a pair of metal workers, and obviously we work with leather and hides. Got a weaver and about ten carpenters, too. Cooks and the like. My cousin is good with wheels and the wagons, and he tinkers with Hightec when we find it," Stanger said, looking at Andi's tablet.

"I can use the help. Good," she said.

I held out my hand. "Will you join us?"

"We will," he said without looking around. He knew a good deal when he heard it, and he wasn't going to waste time. I like that kind of decisiveness.

"Who is your second in command?" I asked.

"My sister, Elsie. She's——"

I turned and waved vaguely to the west. "Out there with a rifle on me. Tell her to come on in."

Stanger fell into stunned silence for a second, then he smiled, abashed. He lifted a thick hand and made a circle with his index finger, and Elsie stood up from her cover some hundred meters away. She was small, pretty, and wearing a broad grin as she slung her rifle and began loping toward us in an easy trot.

"When did you see her?" Stanger asked.

"I didn't, but I also didn't see your second in command, so I figured they were giving you cover," I said. Elsie arrived, not breathing hard and still smiling. She was just over five feet tall and had large, intelligent dark eyes in a pretty face. I thought she looked Persian, but when she spoke, there was a slight drawl to her words.

"He made me right away, but I couldn't signal. She was watching, too," Elsie said, nodding toward Andi.

"Damn. Twice?" Stanger asked.

"Call it a healthy sense of suspicion," Andi said.

"I'd call it good eyes, too," Elsie concluded

before taking a water bottle and drinking deeply. Her neck glistened with sweat, and she wore clothes that were so bland in color I never would have seen her, not unlike the cat that attacked me.

"Now that we know each other a bit better, how will we gain entrance to the, ah, town? I assume you can't just walk up and move in?" Stanger said.

"No, you can't, but we have security in place just for things like this. How many people do you have, in total?" I asked.

"Eighty-three," he answered.

"Okay, Andi? Let's get them catalogued," I said. She stood, swept a finger over her tablet, and inserted a small drive in one of the ports. "We're going to ask the name, skill, and age of everyone in your group, and then we're going to take their picture. You'll take your people south with Breslin as your guide."

"I'm staying with you, Jack. You need three, not two. Hell, you need an entire war party, as far as I'm concerned," Breslin said.

"You would be right, if we were going to war. We're not. This is deep recon and nothing more, and I trust you. Take Stanger and Elsie and their people home, and give Silk the drive. You're in charge of their housing, and ask Silk and Lasser to assign sites based on their crafts. The cattle are another issue entirely. We don't have fencing, and I don't know how to build it without stripping material we need for houses."

"I can help with that," Elsie said.

"I'm listening," I replied, interested in her solution. She was young, but confident and cloaked in an air of competence, like her brother.

"We only have forty head, with about eight calves on the way unless there are twins. We need a small lot for them if we can graze them during the day. They'll need a barn first, but even that can wait if there's cover from the sun," Elsie said.

"There is. We have trees that give shade," I said.

"Okay, then we can set up a wire and pole fence from the stores we have, and if you can find stone and lumber, we put up a low barn, no more than three meters high with a sloped roof," Elsie said, tilting her hand to indicate an angled structure.

"Consider it done. We have ample access to dry timber. The roof might be tricky, but we have a sawmill under construction for planking. It's not ready, but it will be," I said.

"Then we keep the cattle bottled up until it is, and it's no different than how things are now. Fewer threats, I imagine," Elsie said, then her face broke into a grin that made her seem very young. "You really have trees?"

"We do," Andi said. "And ponds, and clean water, and people. You'll be a part of something stable, if that's what you want."

"I do. I mean, we all do. We just—something is wrong out here. Monsters and shit coming around at night, and even in the day, and things I've never seen before. None of us have," Elsie said, concern mixing with relief in her voice.

"We're used to seeing animals flee during the fire season, but there are no fires," Stanger said.

"There's a fire, you just can't see it. It's the virus, and it never stopped working," I said.

"I wish it would rain, then," Elsie said, and I felt myself nod along with her sentiment. Maybe one day we could be the storm that puts the fire out permanently. Until then, we would find safety where we could, and allies whenever possible.

"Me too," Stanger said. He cupped his hands and shouted that everyone should come to us for pictures, earning a few odd looks and some open smiles by people who knew what that meant. Andi began taking their images and asking questions as she built a mini-census of the camp, while Breslin, Stanger, and I looked over their wagons for possible contributions to The Oasis. They had tools, food, and a minor smattering of Hightec, but nothing comparable to what we had tucked away in the Cache.

The census took nearly two hours. We took our time, getting to know the people, because in a few days, they would be *my* people and under my care. I knew the process would have bumps, but giving them a calm word would go a long way toward assuring them that Stanger was making the right move. Andi was a natural in her role, and the kids found Breslin fascinating. By the end of the survey, he had no less than five little ones following him around, asking so many questions he couldn't get a word in edgewise. That occupied his mind, if only for a while, because when he got home he would have to see the source of his betrayal. I hoped time would, at minimum, let him tolerate Jossi's presence, but if it didn't work, then she would be the one leaving, not Breslin. That much I already knew.

When we were done, it was afternoon, right in the sweet spot where animals and kids need a nap.

Even the chickens seemed subdued, sitting in their wide veranda on the wagon, emitting the occasional soft cluck but little else. Stanger was showing me some of the fine points about cattle, and milk, and the giddy fact that we would have dairy products again in The Oasis.

"I haven't asked you this because it's not my concern, but I will now. Where are you going?" Stanger's question was reasonable, given that we were throwing in together to build something.

"I mentioned we were doing recon, but this is the second time we've done it. The first was from the air. We have technology, very old, that lets us fly at considerable altitude. Have you ever seen anything that could fly? Manmade?"

He made a sound of surprise, then shook his head, but stopped in the middle of his motion. "Wait, yes. We saw balloons and a glider, but in the distance. The only reason I knew what we saw was because one of the pilots traded with us, must have been six or seven years ago?"

"Seven," Elsie confirmed. "Up north. Ballsy fucker. He said they launch from a cliff, and the balloons are run on hot air. Craziest thing I'd ever heard, but they were high enough for us to see them on the horizon, at some distance."

I filed that information away, because those were the kind of people we would need when we truly began to expand. "We fly too, but ours are powered by engines, and we have a camera that records our path. We saw some people, far to the northwest, and we're going to make contact."

"The River People?" Elsie asked.

"River? No, more like a forest. Are those the same people?" Andi said.

"I don't know. We met traders on a deep run to the east, said they were going all the way to the biggest river in the world in order to take a ship downstream. Why, I have no idea, because the coast is an absolute killing ground, according to everything we know," Elsie said.

Just like that, our world got bigger.

I cut my eyes at Andi, because I was about to ask a question that might reveal we knew more about the world then we were letting on. Our identity as people from a time before the virus wasn't common knowledge, but it wasn't exactly hidden, either. It was more of a need-to-know basis, but since I was revealing our cache of technology, I decided to let him know the rest.

"Stanger, have you ever heard of technology

from long ago being found? Or, ah—people?" I asked.

He paused, looked at me with a level gaze, and said, "Maybe. Hightec, sure. It's my business, or at least it was until we found cattle and realized they were a lot less dangerous than a collapsing ruin filled with snakes."

"Andi, pull up a tube," I said.

She flicked her fingers, and in seconds, a short video began to play. I was stunned when she leaned forward to show Stanger and his people the screen.

It was Andi. Being put into her tube.

"This is me, about two thousand years ago. I was pumped up with tiny machines and put into suspended animation, and now I'm here, with you," she said.

"Bull. Shit." Stanger crossed his arms, but Elsie gave Andi an odd look.

"Not just me. Jack, too. He went in before I did, and was found by two scavengers working the western Empty. It was dumb luck they found him, but here he is, and here I am, as I said. In the flesh, and better than when I went under. But you don't have to take my word for it. Jack, give me your hand," Andi said.

"Fine. I hope you appreciate this, dammit," I

groused, but I held my arm out. Andi pulled her knife and cut me without hesitation, causing Stanger and his people to leap back, gasp, or both. Once again, only Elsie remained impervious to the event.

"What the fuck are you doing?" Stanger asked, his voice incredulous.

"Watch," Andi said.

So they did. In seconds, the shallow cut began to close, and I flexed my arm, giving Andi a dark look. She grinned and turned her hip to me, as if I were going to spank her. Not really my thing, but for this, I might make an exception.

"They're called nanobots, and there are millions of them in my blood. Tiny machines too small for the human eye to see, developed just before the virus went crazy and burned down what we had for a civilization. Andi has them, too, but because I care for her as a person, I won't cut her with a knife." I smiled toothily at her, and she bowed slightly, then flipped me the bird. "I love you too, dear. As I was saying before my woman— don't look at me like that, you're mine and you know it—decided to use me as a demonstration, the 'bots are what let me sleep all those years. Well, that and the technology of a tube cooled with liquid helium and nuclear power, but those are lectures for the second day of class, so to speak. The point is, Andi and I are from the past, but we're here *now*, and we are going to drag this place kicking and screaming back into civilization whether it wants it or not."

It took a long, awkward moment of silence for my words to sink in, but one by one, I saw faces shift from doubt to questions. That was good.

Elsie spoke first, like I knew she would.

"How many people were put in these tubes?" she asked.

"I don't know. Andi? Dear?" I asked, grinning at her. "Care to chime in on this?"

"I don't know either because we were separated from each other. I was in a . . . facility, by myself, with no one else tubed for redundancy. Usually the military—we had a lot of military back then— loved doing things in twos and threes just to make sure the whole project couldn't be lost. I'd be lying if I didn't think there were more people out there waiting to wake up, but I'm also convinced that not everyone who went into cold sleep survived. Earthquakes, floods, fires; stuff like that would have picked them off here and there no matter how well we were tucked away for our long nap," Andi said.

"And that's where the, ah, computer came from?" Stanger asked.

"This?" Andi held up her tablet. "Yes, but it's not even close to the most important thing we have." She gave me a pointed look, and I nodded. "We have means to power things, and build things, and build more computers, if it comes right down to it. We can fly and shoot and heal, but we can't do it without more people. At first, it's going to be grunt work. All of it, and it's going to suck ass."

"Big time. I was a marine, and most of my life was either waiting or digging or running. Now, we won't be doing any waiting at all. It's *only* work, but the nature of it is changing drastically. In mere months we've built a place that your kids can run around and be safe," I said.

"Kassos," Elsie said, moving forward in our timeline with her question.

"Yes. That's on the list, but not for a while. There's a lot between here and there, if you get me," I said.

"I do, but—even with what you say you can do, Wetterick alone is a big bite," Stanger said. He wasn't dubious, just concerned.

"I agree. I have a lot of reasons to want to stay alive, which is why, when I move on The Outpost, it will be in a way that Wetterick's people will never expect," I said. "I want him gone, but I *don't* want his people killed and buildings torched. We don't have the resources to casually throw away The Outpost without trying to save it for our own."

"Lot of work went into building that place. Not Wetterick, of course, he wouldn't do a damned thing to get dirty, but there were other good people there," Stanger said.

"I know. Lasser is with us, and Silk shares my home," I said.

"Lady Silk? She, ah, used to run her own business there. I know of her," Stanger said carefully.

"She's with me now, and it's okay. I know what she was, and what she owned. The Hannahs are with us now, too," I said.

"She's . . . with you?" Stanger said, cutting his eyes at Andi.

"It's rather crowded in bed, though Mira loves her rifle more than Jack's body. It's rather embarrassing for all of us," Andi said, smiling.

Elsie snorted in delight, while Stanger and everyone else in earshot looked like they would rather be anywhere else.

"I see," Stanger said, though he quite clearly

did not, but he was too experienced to let his face give anything away.

"It's a good place, Stanger. Get going," I said, clasping his arm and smiling.

"Right." He shook himself slightly, perhaps thinking of Silk. I slept with her every night and *still* felt that way. I understood.

I heard a distant call just then, raw and angry, and before anyone could stand except for Andi, I rose, aimed my rifle, and snapped off a shot nearly vertical. Lowering my weapon, I barked, "Everyone back. Incoming."

"What—oh, shit," Stanger said, then began hustling people away from our area.

The dinobird creature hit with a thud, spurting blood from its beak and flopping once, the exit wound from my round evident in the massive hole between its shoulders. "Nasty things. I imagine you have to watch for them with the cattle?"

"Cattle? Try the kids. They'll take anything not tied down, and they're only getting worse," Stanger said. "Nice shot. Now what are we going to do with it?"

I rolled the creature over with the toe of my boot. Its tongue was stiff, deeply veined, and purple, the teeth around it like needles. "We start by firing up your ovens. Who wants dinobird for supper?"

Stanger slipped a well-worn knife from his belt and lifted the animal by its snout. "I could eat."

We did just that, and when the stars came wheeling up, I knew I'd made a good choice with Stanger and his people as I stared into the fire's coals, now cherry red and gray. The day closed soft on all of us for once, and I pulled Breslin aside for another quiet word. He listened, said nothing, and then nodded as the night sounds began to rise on the soft wind. In time, sleep found me, and I put a hand on Andi's hip, her warmth a talisman under my touch.

19

Breslin wasn't happy about acting as an escort, but he understood the importance of his role, so he agreed and made himself comfortable with Stanger's people. I slept under the stars with Andi, wondering what awaited us in the forest.

The forest.

The phrase alone was alien to me after a short time in the rolling open of The Empty, but in truth, I was more curious about what existed *under* the forest. If life itself had been broken apart, then there was no limit to what we could expect. For that reason, taking more people made less sense. Andi and I worked well as a team, and in a pinch, we would be considered a bonded pair, which was true.

"Ready?" I asked her. The only answer was a smile in the dark. The sky was still black, the stars burning bright as a crescent moon hurried away behind the distant horizon, it's job as a guide done for the night.

We moved smoothly to our truck, the only motion around us a pair of sentries who waved quietly. The low murmur of cattle drifted to us from the left, where they were tucked together in a small area between the wagons. Had I not known where and when the scene was taking place, it could have been a typical night in the American west.

But there was nothing typical about our reality, and I took the wheel in hand, turned the power toggle, and drove away north at a crawl, leaving the lights off until we were well away from camp. Andi looked back once, smiling at the sleeping people and cattle, and I knew she felt a sense of peace that they would be brought in from The Empty, where they could thrive.

"That was the best thing that could have happened to us," she said.

"Did you see all the kids? Three pregnant women, too, and even a few dogs with the cattlemen. I feel like I hit the lottery. Twice," I said.

"Three times if you count Mira," she said, earning a bark of laughter from me as I cut the wheel to avoid the form of a collapsed cactus nearly eight meters long. The barrel was a mass of jagged thorns, split open to the sky and already swarmed by insects and small animals eating their fill of the juicy interior.

She brought her tablet to life and began watching a loop of the forest footage, then slowed it down until it was a frame by frame crawl.

"What are you thinking?" I asked her. She was an engineer and did things with a purpose.

"We—the military—never even went to the toilet without a plan. We wouldn't know of the virus without a plan for *after*, if everything went to shit, and so, there must be orders. I'm wondering if we're looking at one of those orders made real," she said.

"The Joint Chiefs left instructions for after the house burned down? I wouldn't put it past them, but this feels like the opposite to me. Like something got even further away from the original intent, mostly due to necessity. Never forget, the sneakiest bastard in the world is a desperate human. It's also the most dangerous animal. Ever.

That woman looks human, but she isn't from our neighborhood," I reasoned.

"Obviously."

"Neither are the animals we're seeing, and if that woman has been underground for any length of time, the world will have changed beyond recognition for her, too. Despite how different we look, we're in the same boat. The world wants us dead, and we both have to figure out a way to survive," I said.

"Common ground. That's a good start." Andi looked at the video again, tracing the outline of the rifle. "For a weapon, it's almost art."

I glanced at the image. She was right. There were sweeping curves along the stock, and what appeared to be a reticule, not sight. The construction had an organic feel to it, like the gun had been grown rather than assembled. I'd seen things like it before, but only in fantasy novels where physics didn't matter.

"Nanobots," I said.

Andi stared at the image, nodding silently. "I think that's it. This wasn't made by human hands. It's machined, but to specs we can't understand. The stock is long, but the barrel is short. You wouldn't have nearly the range for accuracy, but you sure could shoot fast. I don't see a clip, either."

"Look at the stock. Think that could be an internal mag?"

"Huh." She titled the image back and forth, but the resolution could go no higher. "Makes sense. I don't get the feeling this is some antiquated one-shot. Not with this degree of work and design. The color is bizarre, too—it's not wood. I don't know what it is, or even if it's metal at all."

"I guess we'll have to ask her before she uses it on us," I said.

"Are we just going to camp on her site, and see if she pops up like a gopher?"

"It's either that or knock on the door. I'd rather meet her in the open, with a chance to communicate that doesn't seem like an invasion. If I was running defense for a subterranean facility, that's what would keep me calm enough to talk, and I'm betting they have external security. They'll know we're around."

"At least it's a nice spot to camp. I see water," Andi said, pointing to a small ribbon of silver.

"Which means that the land isn't just different than The Empty, it's healthy. Looks like it could be a national park," I said.

"She wore goggles in the vid, so they might be out more at night. I don't think we're going to get much sleep," Andi said, eying the scrolling map on her screen. It was reasonably accurate, being an overlay of our flight data and how things were two thousand years ago. Between the two, we had distance, if not terrain, and I was operating on the idea that the entire route was a shitshow waiting to happen.

"What the fuck happened to the planet, Jack? Not just the ogres and half-assed dinos. The geography is a mess," Andi said, watching the sun rise into an orange rumor, then burst over the horizon with authority. The desert before us was no longer truly desert; it was something like scraggly grasslands, but with broken rock and the occasional tree fighting for height.

"We saw the satellite data, but that doesn't tell us how bad it was here on the ground. I'm guessing earthquakes had a lot to do with it, but storms, too, and then a lack of humanity to moderate things. There would be enormous, unchecked fires from lightning and the dry season. We changed this place, and when we were gone, nature changed it back."

"But new rivers? Where did they come from?

In twenty centuries? There weren't even that many rivers in Oklahoma to begin with, and a lot of those were just glorified creeks. I've seen at least four rivers that would be a bitch to cross, and not one of them is on any topo map from our time," Andi said.

"We need a geologist for that one, I think, but at least one of those rivers was made by an earthquake. When we were turning west on our second leg of the recon, there was a massive cliff that hadn't been worn by the wind or rain. That's new, at least in geological terms, so there's one piece of evidence. But that makes me wonder how the woman with the gun has lived underground all this time. If there is that much activity in the earth, it would play hell on any civilization under the surface. Doesn't make sense, at least not to me."

I slowed as we passed the enormous ribs of an animal, stripped of flesh and bleached white by the sun. They were two meters long and scored by countless small teeth. In the shadow of the pelvis, a wild dog and her pups took cover from the rising sun as she nursed them. Life went on, even in the physical shadow of death, and the mother dog bared her teeth at the truck, protective even in the face of something fifty times her size.

We picked our way at five klicks an hour, following no path as I avoided everything larger than a baseball. The truck had solid tires and a suspension built for rock crawling, but even so, I knew we had few replacement parts on hand, and a long way to walk if we broke down because I decided to hurry. As the sun rose, the day grew warm, then hot, and then it was directly overhead in a brilliant globe that told me it was time to stop, eat, and take our bearings.

We made our temporary camp in sight of a sinkhole ringed by low scrub trees. The trees had a variety of birds calling in raucous voices that alerted anything in the area to our presence. We put a small canopy up on the roof and sat cross-legged, eating cold roots and salted pork in contented silence.

"Even when barbecue is cold, it's good," Andi said.

"Amen." I swigged from a waterskin and handed it to her, watching the area for any activity. Since it was the heat of day, not much was going on, but after almost getting turned into a two-hundred-pound cat toy, I was on my best behavior.

"What's your estimate on our time?" I asked when we were done eating. Andi grabbed her tablet and flicked through a few maps, settling on one that compared known data points with what we had already traveled.

"We're here," she said, touching the screen, "and we need to go here. I'd say we have nine hours of light left, and if we follow this stream bed —not that one, the one over here—then we pick up enough time to arrive before dark."

"I can push it a bit, if we leave right now. Those two flat spots will be easy rolling," I said, jumping down from the roof and holding out my hand. She took it, then dragged the canopy down and folded the flexible frame up in two motions, sliding it behind the seats.

I started the truck and we accelerated away to the cries of the birds, who were happy to see us go. Even in a place that had once been my home state, I still didn't feel welcome sometimes.

20

WE STOPPED two more times during the trip, once for a bathroom break while I kept yelling at Andi that there were snakes eyeballing the perfect pear of her bum. Naturally, she didn't find me as hilarious as I found myself, so I was content to ride in silence while she rubbed her leg where she fell into some dry grass. After I offered her a drink of whiskey, she forgave me, smiled, and pointed to the north with gusto.

"On, Jeeves!" she shouted, and for a moment, life was as normal as it could be in my fallen world.

Then we saw a cloud of dust, so I slowed before driving into it. Our third stop of the day was caused by a herd of bison, their huge heads low, dark horns gleaming in the sun. They were half again as large as the ones I'd seen in Colorado during my youth, with shoulders a meter and a half across and muscles on top of muscles.

"Are those . . . regular sized buffalo?" Andi had asked. I told her no, we watched in stunned awe, and after ten minutes, the herd of about a thousand or more of the beasts had gone past us, heading east at a modest walk. I guessed they weren't in much of a hurry because there were few predators willing to challenge them in a group that size. There was something to be said for security in numbers, just like my plans for The Oasis.

Other than the bison, we saw birds, lizards, and an array of creatures that flashed away at first sight of our truck, their instincts keeping them at maximum distance to us. After a short detour around a minor washout, we caught a break. A game trail—probably from the bison—led in the general direction of our goal, and we followed it at a smooth fifteen klicks, even brushing higher speeds for short distances where the animals had pummeled the land into something like a primitive roadway.

With less than an hour of light left and my nerves starting to fray, I saw the tops of trees at the absolute limit of my vision. "We're here. Or almost here."

Andi checked her map. "Close. Pull right in the driveway, so to speak?"

"We will. I want the truck close, and we're sleeping on top tonight. If there's water and food in this forest, then there are predators, and they have the advantage of cover here. I haven't seen giant scorpions out in the open, but we know they're around. I'm not taking that chance," I said, turning the wheel to leave the path and cut across grass that grew thicker and clumpier, broken by occasional flowers. Within moments, we were edging toward a slight incline, topped with an actual green forest.

"Do you smell that?" I asked. Our windows were down, and the air was clean.

"It's—water?" Andi said.

"Life. Not a desert. This is how The Oasis might be, if we can continue expanding and finding an aquifer that goes onward. This is our future, Andi. Right here," I said. I could hear the excitement in my voice. It was like a time machine, and the vision was five years from now if we played our cards right and didn't lose to nature. It was a huge if, but seeing the forest made it seem possible.

"It's beautiful. I wish Mira and Silk could see this," she said dreamily. "Especially Mira, after all the shit she had to go through just to eat."

"Silk didn't have it easy, you know."

"I know. I didn't mean to make it sound like that. I know she had a shitty life, too, in her own way. But Mira was out *in* The Empty, and she was a kid. She's still young, you know?" Andi said.

"She's tough as nails and she's healing," I said. I believed every word of it, too. We didn't need fake nice, not in our world. Not in our family.

"She is, and I can see she's getting less guarded. Still, I would like them to see this. If it goes well, that is," Andi said, then looked down at her tablet. "Left, see that tall pine, or whatever it is? The door is in front of it. Huh. Notice anything about that tree?"

I stopped the truck, peering up at the towering pine. There was something wrong with it. Then it *clicked* in my vision. "It's not a tree. It's an antenna."

"I'll be damned," Andi said. "It's a fake. The limbs are antenna, too. It's taller than anything else, so it has a clear broadcast path, but to what?"

"Let's ask the lady of the forest when she comes out for a stroll," I said, pulling us forward until we were less than thirty meters from the doorway. "About here, I think. Welcome to Forward Base Oasis."

"Delighted," Andi said, drawing her weapon and opening the truck door. I did the same. Climbing on top of the truck, we took a look around. The place was green, lively, and damp in some spots where the sun was kept from the ground. There were areas that seemed darker green, and then places where flowers grew in abandon. Trees climbed toward the sun, vines climbed some of the trees, and everywhere, birds chittered and called as they wrapped up the business of the day, finding their roosts until daybreak. It was paradise, and it gave me hope that we really could save a piece of the world for my people.

"Canopy or no?" Andi asked.

"Not tonight. We need maximum vision in here," I said with a shake of my head. "When you get down off the truck, I do too. We stay together at all times."

"If you think I'm wandering off like some dipshit girl in a horror film, you need to pay more attention to my habits. I'm stuck on you tonight, buddy," she said with an emphatic slash of her hand.

"Good. Let's eat and settle in. Gonna be a long night, and I have a feeling we won't be alone for long," I said.

We broke out more food, nibbling idly despite our hunger. The forest was *noisy*, though I knew many of the sounds. There was the distant shriek of a fox, coyotes to the west, and something that sounded like a small tank, which turned out to be an armadillo the size of a washing machine. It stopped close enough to us that we could see the starlight gleaming off its back as it rooted for something, snuffled, and then moved on having gouged the earth like a small tractor blade.

"I never knew there was so much activity at night," Andi whispered.

"More than the day. Tough place to be a bug, or a mouse, for that matter. Everything is eating everything else."

"Hope we stay out of that cycle," she said.

"We will. Get some sleep, I'm okay listening. I'll wake you if anything happens."

"Okay." She kissed me and stretched out, pulling a light blanket over herself. In seconds, she was asleep, her breath coming in a steady rhythm like the waves on a lakeshore, soft and soothing. The sky lit with stars over us, and I spent some time picking out constellations and planets, marveling at the lurid colors of the sky in a world where mankind held no sway.

The forest went about its business as if we weren't there, and somewhere in the night, I finally heard the noise I had been waiting for.

I heard . . . nothing.

No animals. No birds. Nothing. A hole in the sounds of the forest, moving left to right as the animals fell silent while someone or something moved among them, slow, steady, and without a single hint of noise. As stalking went, it was masterful, and I kept my eyes averted from the direction in which we were being watched. I didn't freeze. I kept breathing, moving, adjusting myself with all the little twitches of someone who is fighting boredom and the night for a long watch.

And then the forest came back to life as if it had never gone silent.

"Huh. Slick," I murmured. Whoever had been there was gone, and it would be morning before I could investigate. I waited until the sky began to grow light in the east, sparing Andi her pointless watch, then I settled next to her, pulled her body to mine, and slept.

21

"IT'S DAYLIGHT," Andi said in my ear, and I recalled one of my life lessons that I'd forgotten since coming out of the tube. The only thing worse than no sleep is one hour of sleep.

"It is. Also, I'm dead."

"You're not dead, but your breath is," she said, smiling and handing me a cup. "Drink this."

"What is it?" I asked, levering myself up with a mild groan. My 'bots were already going to work on my lingering fatigue, but even they had limits.

"Cold brew coffee with double caffeine," she said.

I jolted up. "Coffee?" Where the fuck did you get—"

She dissolved into laughter, then patted my cheek. "Just fucking with you. We have no coffee, because the gods hate us, and also, we're in the future, where people are in hell because there is no coffee."

"That's a dirty ass trick. And now I'm awake because of false hopes and lingering anger."

"Mission accomplished. You're welcome," she said. "Why didn't you wake me for my watch?"

"No point." I drained the cup and wiped my mouth. "Our host was here, but she left, and I knew she wasn't coming back. After a while, I figured I'd catch a little shuteye with you. Very little, as it turned out."

"She was here? How do you know?" Andi asked, breathless.

"The forest went quiet. You can hide from people, but you can't hide from the animals. Something moved through verrrryy slowly, and very carefully, too. It wasn't what I heard, it was what was missing. I tracked it—or her, I think—and we can check it out today, in the safety of sunlight," I explained.

"What are we waiting for? Show me," Andi said, but I sat, unmoving.

"I'm hungry, and we're going to eat first. Then, we go to ground with our eyes open, and ready," I said.

"Okay. Since you're being so reasonable. Never thought I would be the second most responsible person in this outfit," she said with a laugh. We ate slowly, watching our surroundings as the sun began to break through the trees in rays that looked solid enough to walk on. It was a stunning display of natural wonder, far different from the stark nature of The Empty.

For the first time since I woke up, I saw butter-flies, even though they were twice as big as any in my time. I heard the hum of insects, chirping birds, and the startled squawk of something that became breakfast for something else. It was a living forest, and I knew we had a long way to go at The Oasis.

"Ready?" I asked when we broke from our moment of quiet.

"Ready," she said, following me down to land light on her feet.

We unstrapped our guns and began to walk in a roundabout way, cautious of traps, and animals, and hazards. I knew the ground looked stable, but I didn't want a broken leg due to a fiendish gopher who thought the forest was the best place for his home. We took our time with each step, spiraling outward from the truck but always in sight of it. There was no need for talking, because we were both too busy watching our surroundings.

What surroundings we saw. I was stunned by the array if insects, squirrels, and other small critters that fled with angry squeaks when we stepped into their small home range. There was a healthy bed of moss—the first I'd seen—and flowering plants that were just on the edge of recognition for me, like they had once been something I knew.

I held up my hand and we stopped a couple meters from something that didn't fit with the rest of the scene. Five rocks were piled on top of each other in a stack, the rocks descending in size as they went up. The balance was perfect, and there was something metallic on the top rock, shadowed by the low limb of a tree with small, bright leaves.

"See it?" I asked.

Andi nodded.

"I'll approach. You back up in case—well, in case of anything, really." I started to walk forward and froze again, this time pointing down with my rifle barrel. "Look."

"Edge of a print," Andi said, crouching to examine the smear on a flat rock where moss had been moved to one side. It was a human track, and there was a second nearby. Other than that, we saw no evidence of people. It was as if they had emerged form thin air, built the tiny rock cairn, and vanished.

"I'm going forward," I said. I circled toward the back side of the tree, looking around at the rocks. Then I laughed, causing Andi to lift her shoulders and hands in a universal *what the fuck is going on* gesture.

I reached over and lifted the shiny object, holding it up so Andi could see. It was a chain, and on the end was a key. There was something else, too. I pushed through the limb and reached alongside the rocks. "Andi, come check this out."

She approached carefully, then her face registered naked shock when she could see the entire scene. "What the hell?"

Two glasses and a small bottle of something that looked a *lot* like booze sat on a flat rock just beside the cairn. I picked up the bottle, careful of my own health, pulled the small cork, and took an experimental sniff. "I'm no expert, but I'd swear that was rum, or something close to it."

"Great. We have underground pirates. Now what?" she said.

I looked at the key, and the glasses, and the bottle. "I think they're inviting us down for a drink. Who are we to say no?"

22

"I DON'T KNOW about this, Jack. I like adventure and all, but I'm not sure that going back to their place on the first date is a good idea, if you know what I mean," Andi said, eying the glasses and bottle warily.

"I agree. It wouldn't be the best move to walk in there right now."

"You agree?" She narrowed her eyes at me, then waved her hand, asking me for the rest of my thought.

"We wait until closer to noon, and *then* we turn the key and go see our new friends. Makes a lot more sense that way," I said.

"Huh. The sun," Andi said.

"Right. It will fill the opening and give us an

advantage, at least for a second. If they're hostile, we can withdraw and make them fight their way out. If they're friendly, we get a chance to show them we're cautious, and we get a good look at them first. I don't want any surprises, but if they were able to get within thirty meters of the truck without me seeing them, then it would have been a simple matter to pop both of us with one of the those rifles we saw the woman carrying. I think they mean to talk, because we're still breathing," I concluded.

"Okay, we wait until high noon. I feel like I'm in an old western," Andi said with a grin. "Except for the whole underground-pod-people thing, of course."

"Yeah, that's kind of against the grain for westerns. But who knows, they have rifles. Might have hats, too, we just need to wait a bit and see," I said as we walked back to the truck and climbed up. I began getting my pack together as Andi did the same, then we went to the nearest stream, filled our waterksins, ate, and watched the hawk-sized butterflies for a while as the sun rose above us until it pierced the forest canopy like darts of golden thread. When the lines of light were nearly overhead, I stood up, offered my hand to Andi, and pulled her to her feet.

"I hope they're still like us," she said.

"I hope they aren't. Look what happened to our world, and then look at this one," I said, jumping down and adjusting my pack. I had my blades, rifle, and knives all close to hand, but my instincts told me there was more to this meeting than potential conflict. This was the point we'd been working toward since waking, a place in our history we could one day look back on with pride. We found an ally, we built something, and we began reclaiming our world even beyond the borders of The Oasis.

"Shall we?" I asked.

Andi bowed and we walked, side by side to the hidden doorway set cleverly into the ground. It was a masterwork of stealth engineering, and I didn't see a keyhole until we were kneeling by the door.

"I'll be damned." I lifted a small patch of moss that was slightly different in color, and there was the lock. It wasn't metal. "What material is that?"

"Ceramic, but maybe a hybrid of some kind. It's not like anything we could make. Looks a bit like the outer shell they used on the comet lander in '29." Andi was examining the lock, then she shrugged. "It's a lock. You have a key. Seems simple enough from here."

"Okay. Knock, knock," I said, inserting the key without hesitation. The lock clicked inward, rotated ninety degrees, and then . . . nothing.

Andi pointed to the moss that grew at the edge of the fake stone. "It's moving."

The door moved a tiny amount, and then swung inward and recessed to the left in complete silence. The air that came out was cool, fresh, and smelled alive, not musty or stale. Sunlight poured past our shoulders in a blaze, lighting up the steps that descended for two meters and then ended abruptly at another door, emblazoned with the symbol **EC-1**.

"Well, there's your confirmation about the Eden Chain being real," I said.

Andi grunted, taking in the scene with the eyes of an engineer. I saw a chokepoint that was bad for combat, but she saw something else. "It's an airlock."

"No shit. It is," I said, noting the cleanliness of the steps, and walls, and even the complete lack of water. Whatever I'd been expecting, this wasn't it.

"They have an airlock, so there must be a way to cycle it from inside, unless—" Andi looked around, then reached back and removed the key. "Yeah, here it is. Look—this key has two sides. I bet the airlock is triggered by the second side. It's a kind of failsafe. You might force your way through that stone door, but I bet the airlock is military grade, and even if you *did* get through—"

"They have guns on the other side in a perfect killbox. This is American, all right," I said.

"If there's an airlock, then there must be other fake trees up top, I bet. They need a way to cycle fresh air through here, and the best way would be something you couldn't compromise with a nerve agent or smoke, just by tossing a grenade into it. Have to be tall, like that antenna," Andi said.

The inner door clanged, and we both pointed our rifles at it without thinking. Then a panel on the airlock recessed to reveal a wheel lock, not unlike ships used to close off sections during a hull breach.

I stood there with the sun streaming down, staring at the wheel and knowing that I had to spin it. I had to open the door and find out what was on the other side. Andi knew it too.

Without a word, I reached back and pulled the outer door closed, ending the daylight with a shrinking stripe of light that went dark when the door whooshed into place. We stood in the dark for a moment, letting our eyes adjust while our 'bots worked feverishly to help. When I no longer had floaters in my vision, I began to notice a soft amber glow around the inner hatch. A second glow leaked through the panel where the wheel extended, so I moved forward, grabbed the wheel, and turned. It spun easily in my hands, the mechanism silent and smooth. I had not met these people from under the forest yet, but I already respected the way they took care of things. That was a good sign.

A soft hiss of air blew out from overpressure, and the scent of a pine forest filled my nose. "Pine trees?"

"Um . . . yeah," Andi said into the dark. She reached out and looped a hand under my bicep, and I pulled her closer to me before pushing the hatch inward. It swung *up*, not to the side, and the pull had the distinct feel of a magnetic piston.

The woman from the forest was waiting for us, a smile on her face and a glass in one hand. "I'm glad you joined me for that drink."

23

Before I said a word, I took stock of the woman before us, because she was easily the most exotic female I'd ever seen. Even Andi was quiet, regarding the beautiful woman with an expression of curious delight.

Our host's smile deepened, revealing white teeth framed by pink lips. Her eyes were a blue so pale they seemed gray, and she had high cheekbones, long, fine blonde hair, and a tall, athletic frame that was thin without being skinny. She was alabaster white, and wore a dark red tunic tucked into blue leggings and boots. It wasn't a uniform, but it came close, being free of adornment except for an oval necklace that looked like silver. At her hip, she carried a strange latch with a handle grip, and a knife protruded from a thigh scabbard. As combat rigs go, it was the most unusual setup I'd ever seen. Her rifle was nowhere to be seen, but her goggles were pushed up on her head as if she anticipated going outside. *Interesting*.

"Is it rum?" I asked. "I was always a whiskey man, unless I was on a boat. Then I felt compelled to drink rum. Must be latent pirate genes, I said, stepping into the gloom. "Jack—"

"Bowman, we know. And this is Andi, though I suspect your name is Andrea, in the old style?" she said, stepping forward and holding out her hand.

I shook it, trying to keep the surprise off my face and failing. She took Andi's hand as I watched, then turned to me, holding the glass up with a quirked brow. "Aristine, First General of the Eden Chain. Let's talk."

We went down a series of stairs until we reached a clean, open room with low light and an actual wooden table and chairs. The craftsmanship was incredible, and I ran my fingers over the wood in appreciation while Aristine filled glasses with rum, then got taller glasses from a recessed cabinet. She opened a hidden refrigerator, pulled out a pitcher of water and ice, and poured us a round of that as well. It was the most civilized act I'd seen since the first time I met Silk, and every motion of Aristine's long fingers reminded me of all the things that we lost when the world died.

"To rekindled dreams," Aristine said, clinking my glass, and then Andi's.

We sipped the rum, and I closed my eyes as the flavor filled my mind with memory. "This is . . . far better than what I've had since, ah, my awakening. But I feel like you know that for some reason?"

Aristine smiled, but there was no malice. "We have extensive listening devices and cameras throughout the forest, so that's how I know your name. As to the nature of your age, I can surmise that you—and Andi—are not residents of The Empty."

"Good thing I was on my best behavior out there," I said, earning a grin from Andi.

"You both showed an unusual respect for the land, which is something we needed to know before we revealed ourselves. Your recon flight was timely. I don't go topside during the day very often, but we were collecting data on herd movements when you flew overhead," Aristine said.

"Why do I get the feeling this is a waiting room?" Andi asked.

"Astute of you, Andi. What is your training, if I may?" Aristine said.

"Engineer. I was one of the primaries on Fortress: Cache, and then I went under just before the shit hit the fan, so to speak," Andi said.

"And Jack, you were under as well?" Aristine asked.

I nodded, still marveling at the rum. "I was. I went under before her and was found by two scavengers. If not for them, I'd either be dead or sleeping, depending on how long the power lasted at my site."

Aristine nodded gravely in the way of someone who understood how dicey luck could be.

I leaned forward on the table, choosing my words carefully. "Are you alone?"

Aristine laughed, then turned her glass as she considered how to answer. "I haven't been alone for a moment since birth, Jack, but I respect your question. Wait—I was technically alone while collecting data topside, during your flyover, but here in the Chain, there's very little in the way of loneliness. You have the look of serious people. Are you rebuilding, and that's why you chose to fly this way?"

"We are. Almost three hundred as of now, and

growing. I call it The Free Oasis, and we've got good water, a small holdover facility, and then I found Andi. I'm sure you know what that meant in terms of tech and support structure," I said.

"Reactors?" Aristine asked with interest.

"Many. And Vampires, which you saw, drones, printers, and enough hardware to reclaim half of the desert. We're doing it slowly by planting gene-tweaked seeds for a fast canopy. We're tapping wells and running channels outward, building a sort of planned city in hopes that we can stabilize the region. For now," I added.

"And you were looking north for more land?" Aristine asked in a neutral tone.

"Not at all. We were looking for threats. There's something wrong up there, and I don't know what it is. Animals that have been dead since before the last Ice Age are wandering around now, and I need to know why. That's *one* of our issues," I said.

"We also have a local warlord with designs on our people. That has to be dealt with before we can move forward with our other plans," Andi said.

"Which are?" Aristine sipped her water, watching us above the rim of her glass. It was difficult not to stare at her. She was like a statue made real.

"I'm going to rebuild civilization," I said.

A quiet hum settled over the table as Aristine considered my blunt goal. "That's rather aggressive."

"I'm an aggressive person. I have no tolerance for keeping slaves, or the abuse of demi-humans, or allowing shitheads like Wetterick to rule over their little kingdoms without any consequences," I said.

"And you intend to replace them with . . . yourself?" Aristine asked, arching a brow. The hint of a smile curved her lips, and I tipped my glass toward her.

"A fair concern. I can only be better than them, not perfect, but I *will* install the rule of law, and we *will* have a free society. We either build it that way, or not at all," I said.

Aristine nodded with the air of someone making an important decision, letting her eyes lose focus as she stared down.

I took in every inch of her features, uniform, and general beauty as she sat in silence. Even though I felt myself staring, I didn't stop.

Without turning her head, Aristine spoke. "You

find me beautiful, Jack. That's only natural, because I *am* beautiful. So is Andi. Even now, sitting this close to me, I can smell your desire for her." She turned to regard Andi with a sunny smile. "Does that make you happy, knowing that he has an attraction for you, even now in the presence of another woman?"

Andi laughed, then tilted her head to Aristine. "How long have you been underground, girl? He's a man, and quite a specimen, at that. I am not, ah, his *only* woman." She turned to me, shaking her head. "If my college professors heard me say *that*, they would have had me committed."

"Don't hate me because I'm beautiful," I said with a dignified sniff.

Aristine laughed too. "I did not think that topsiders could value survival over tradition, and yet, here it is. You surprise me, Andi, and in the best way possible. As a commander, I have petty jealousies and intrigue to deal with on a daily basis, even here in the Chain. One would think that two thousand years of practice would free us of these archaic issues, but men are men and women are women, even here." She shrugged, powerless to overcome the influence of hormones.

"You call this place the Chain, but weren't

there many locations? I thought the Department of Defense had as many as six distinct bolt holes ready to go in the area," Andi said.

"There were. Six, that is, but they were far more than just a bolt hole. The contingency plans took into account a variety of ways that humanity would kill itself off. There were protocols for everything from nuclear exchange to a comet strike, but the virus was far worse than both of those because no one knew what would be left over. Scavengers are one thing, but an array of new and terrible predators, diseases, and landscapes was more than even we were prepared for. And no one was prepared like us. You'll see," Aristine said.

"You said there *were* six locations in the Chain. What happened to them?" I asked.

Aristine gave me a half-smile, then stood. "They're still here, and I'd like to show you."

24

SHE LED us into a wide hallway with low lighting, the walls painted dark. It was silent, cool, and scented with hints of life, far different than any other place I had been since exploring the ruins of my world. After ten meters, we stood before a massive double door with a small screen in the center right at eye level. Aristine was easily six feet tall, and when she stepped up to the panel, she leaned close as a blue light scanned her iris.

"I have a question before we go any further," I said when she pulled away from the scanner. A soft click echoed through the hallway, and Aristine put a long finger on the door near a small circle of metal I hadn't seen before.

"Ask, and I will answer," the woman said placidly. She faced us both, waiting.

"Your people have been underground for two thousand years?"

"Give or take, but yes, we have," she answered.

Andi whistled softly as if confirming this made her engineer's mind go haywire. The logistics alone were baffling, let alone the details of actually surviving under the surface for that long.

"Would you say you're representative of your people?" I asked.

Aristine lifted a brow, but her lips played at a smile. "There is nothing about me that is average, or I would not have been elected First General, but, yes. I am of the Chain, and I look like it. Why?"

"Forgive me for this, but I thought you would be shorter," I said, looking pointedly at our surroundings.

Understanding dawned on Aristine's face, and she nodded, then turned to push the button on the door. "That's not unreasonable, given your assumptions about our environment. Once you're inside, though, I think you'll understand that we are not, in fact, a dwarven race skulking about in the dark."

The doors swung inward, then recessed, and a light wind of fresh forest air bathed my face as if I was standing outside, among the trees.

Andi gasped, and I felt my jaw drop before reminding myself to close it. Before us, an entire world opened, filled with tall pines, and redwood, and oak trees that sprawled and climbed and stretched like they were trying to grow to heaven. Walkways went from tree to tree, and there were homes and runways and hanging globes of light, obscured by the flitting birds that moved about in constant motion. The houses looked organic, as if they were a part of the landscape, with wide windows and porches that wrapped all the way around. Far below, I saw paths, the silver ribbon of a stream, and the distinct rows of crops, winding along the bottom of the space in green profusion. To my utter shock, a horse walked below, ridden by a young boy who towed a friend in a wagon with blinking lights. Everywhere, there was quiet purpose, bursts of laughter, and lilting whistles that I knew to be a kind of call between people at some distance.

My eyes were drawn to the ceiling, a dark space lit with long, odd tubes that were whipcord thin and subject to wild changes of direction.

Aristine grinned, then took my hand and pulled me forward into her world. "If we were to be called anything other than human, I would call us elves."

We descended by a walkway that was attached to the wall, then veered at a long, sloping angle, touching the trunks of two redwoods before contacting the ground. What lay beneath my feet was no floor. It was land, or something quite close to it, covered with moss and grass, broken by rows of crops and the occasional circle of blackberry brambles. Looking back up at where we came from, the lighted tubes along the ceiling seemed brighter, casting a glow that was dim but just bright enough to see.

I leaned out to touch an unidentified tree, its trunk wider than our truck. "How old are these?"

Aristine's smile was patient, as she anticipated a barrage of questions. "Since the beginning. These were planted before the virus broke free, grown to saplings, and then transferred here when the end was in sight."

"How do they grow in this light?' Andi asked.

"The same way your forest is growing in brutal heat. They're genetic tweaks, done well before the virus was designed. The geneticists started small, so to speak, working in botany before any animal testing. Your facility is one such location. There were twelve in the old United States, and nearly a dozen across the globe. Wherever those facilities were, there is a better chance that the area survives to this day," Aristine said.

I thought of something I'd heard before, bringing a question to mind. "Durban, South Africa?"

"One of the facilities was there, yes. Did it survive the fall?" Aristine asked. "We have mixed information."

"I think so, but my knowledge is second or third hand at best. Silk—that's one of my, ah—" I started, but Andi jumped in.

"One of his other women used to run a whorehouse, and she charmed men out of drive wedges with enough history on them to kill a rhino. We've been culling them for some time," Andi said.

"I see," Aristine said with genuine interest. "These drives, were they formatted *after* the virus hit?"

"Quite likely. We're willing to share, if only because compiling them eats up too much time at the Cache. We'd rather be building than sifting the past," I said.

"We can revisit that later, after you make your decisions about how we should interact," Aristine said.

"Our decision? It's yours as well. We're not pirates, nor will we ever be," I said.

"I'm glad to hear it. In that case, we have much to see, and not a great deal of time before your Oasis comes under attack. You came here to talk, and now, we are in my home. What is it that you wish to know?" Aristine asked, her voice serene. Overhead, a jay was haranguing someone for something, because no matter what year it was, bluejays were assholes.

"For starters," I said, "everything."

25

WE SAT in Aristine's command center, which was also her home. It was low, wide, and airy, given that there was no weather to contend with, and privacy didn't seem to be a major concern among her people. Her house straddled a walkway and a redwood of such size that it didn't even seem real, with bark creases deep enough to hide inside. A young woman and two middle aged men joined us, silently depositing two trays of food and drinks before leaving to hover on the porch, their ears fairly swelling with the effort to hear our conversation.

"Staffers, or family?" I asked.

"Both, given that we're all related. I wanted your first day here to be low impact, since so much of what you will see and hear might be a bit . . . overwhelming," Aristine said, pouring something that smelled quite like wine.

At my raised brow, she gave a musical laugh, then handed cups to Andi and me. "We may live underground, but we're not animals, and several grapes do rather well on the slopes of trees. It's a— micro-micro climate, you might say. Each vine produces something a bit different," Aristine said.

"What don't you have down here?" Andi asked.

Aristine's face went blank, but then she smiled, if a bit tightly. "We'll get to that. But first, the big things."

"The big things, yes," I said, leaning forward.

"You asked what happened to the other parts of the Chain. The answer is simple. They are here, connected to us, and we are now a single unit, for reasons I'm sure you can understand, and perhaps some you cannot," Aristine said.

"Security in numbers," I said. When Aristine nodded, I went on. "Which means you have threats, which means that even under here, you have had to fight to live."

"Indeed. We also face an unstable earth. A rockslide took nearly twenty percent of Eden Four a century ago, and we have only just recovered. It's a good life, but a life made on balance, not excess. For that reason, we have crews that go to the surface, because we are, after all, human, and it is our mission to see to it that the earth survives. That people survive, and not just down here. Up there, too," Aristine said, pointing skyward.

"Why do you go out? Into the world?" I asked.

"To save what we can from the old world, for one thing. Eden Six has a museum three times the size of the old Louvre, and we're expanding it," Aristine answered.

"That is—what have you saved?" Andi asked, each word urgent.

"You'll get to see, but suffice it to say there are things from your world and the time well past American history. There have been *dozens* of empires over the years, rising and falling like the tides, and always leaving something behind in their ashes. They almost always end in fire, but we save what we can. As to the other reasons why we leave here, there are scientific considerations. We bring animals in, and plants, and we continue to release augmented species that may help humanity, but always quietly, and in the dark of night," Aristine explained.

"Like the Indricothere and the giant snakes?" I

asked. If that was the policy of the Chain, then we needed to have a serious discussion about their concept of *helping*.

"Indricothere? You mean the giant—well, it was a rhino, was it not? I confess, biology is not my strong suit, though I recognize the term from our museum. We have many of the fossils from collections across the world, but we would never release an animal of that size. Why would we?" Aristine asked, bewildered.

"Why, indeed, and yet they're roaming free in The Empty, after not having been alive for tens of millions of years. It's not just them, it's a massive array of species, all deadly in some sense or another, though some are simply giant herbivores. As to humanity, the ogres are evidence enough for me that the virus did a lot of dirty work, and continues to do so," I said.

"The human genome is a broken ladder now. There are as many examples of devolution as there are evolution, and we're seeing things that are completely new to the saltiest people working in The Empty," Andi said.

"New animals," Aristine mused, turning away to a cabinet. She withdrew a gray scroll and rolled it out on an artist's table. "Come, look at this."

She tapped the inert gray paper and it flickered to life. It was neither scroll nor paper, but a screen.

"Holy shit," Andi said. "You did it. We barely had this working, but you—you never stopped developing things down here, did you?"

"We did not, and we have no intention of doing so. Our lives are made simpler by the most complex technology that has ever existed, but in our limited area, discoveries come slowly. We improved upon some ideas, went in new directions. We even dove into exotic math, taking our time to explore every detail of a problem until we had a solution that would make something better, not just different." Aristine hefted her rifle, holding it out for me.

"It's almost weightless," I said in wonder. It couldn't have weighed a full kilo, and yet I knew it was loaded.

"Composite extrusions from our printers. A ceramic wafer stronger than steel, capable of dispersing any shock, and durable enough to use as a club. It fires almost frictionless rounds accurate to a range of a kilometer, given a fair wind and low humidity. We do not take pride in killing, but it's a job, and thus, we *will* do it well," Aristine said.

Andi looked at the rifle with new respect. "If

that rifle could tell me I have pretty hair, I'd marry it."

"We'll see what we can do," Aristine said with a laugh. "Our Daymares carry these, and so does the high command. As to weapons, we're all armed, but the long range isn't as necessary down here."

"Daymares?" I asked.

"At any time, we have a squad of six soldiers living topside for an extended period of time. They —ah, *harden* to the conditions up there, and are ready to fight or carry out longer missions at a moment's notice," Aristine said.

"Hence the goggles," Andi said. "I noticed they have multiple settings."

"You are a true engineer, Andi. They do have settings, and over time, the Daymares work to normalize their sight for daytime work, although we obviously prefer working at night. When a night mission is required, we use soldiers who are not acclimated to the sun. Their natural—do you know the word rhodopsin?" Aristine asked.

"No, sorry," Andi said. I stayed quiet as well. The term was Greek to me.

"It's a protein in the eye. We have selected for it over the years, and now, our vision in low light is superb. When it comes to night fighting on the surface, we are without equal, which is one of the reasons no one know of our existence. We aren't seen, or heard, and we never leave anything behind. We work during the dead hours, when the mind of a topsider is tired and sleep is deepest. We are wraiths, and we use this ability only when the situation calls for violence," Aristine said.

"And you don't want to be tracked back here," I added.

"Exactly. It's difficult enough varying the Daymares' paths when they return from a mission, and we consider *any* attention to be a negative," Aristine emphasized.

"What about us? This is attention," I said.

"Yes, but you saw us from a powered flight. We have seen nothing of that for centuries, and there are other issues that must be seen to, lest we drift farther away from the planet that made us. I *am* human, and a woman. I am also a general trying to make peace with the needs of my people, and I must tell you, it isn't easy. We've been self-sufficient for so long, I find the idea of alliances to be unsettling," Aristine admitted.

"Alliances. An interesting choice of words," I remarked drily.

"Is it?" Aristine asked, watching us both carefully.

"Open ended. It implies further help and working together on something that you need as much as we do. Since we need everything, the work could be anything. Sound about right?" I asked.

"It does," Aristine said in a tone so neutral, it seemed like she was a robot. She was cagey.

"Ordinarily, I'd jump at the chance to form an alliance, especially with someone who hasn't begun to show us her cards, in the parlance of my time," I said.

"I'm familiar with the term. Poker lives on down here, you'll be happy to know," Aristine said.

That did make me happy, if only because it conjured nights with my buddies a long time ago. I cleared the memory and refocused on Aristine. "The issue is something you said a moment ago. You called people who live up there *topsiders*, and it's my idea that I don't trust anyone who uses a word that means 'not like me'. That make sense to you?" I asked.

Aristine grew quiet, then nodded. "It does. I mean no harm, but—we *are* different. Are we not?"

"Yes," Andi interjected. "How different?"

"Think of our science, war, natural loss, and

medicines. Two *thousand* years down here in what you might think is paradise, but it's a daily fight to survive because the system, while stable, can be toppled. Jack, nothing would please me more than to rebuild something I only know from vids and lost objects. Now, we have you, and Andi, and a direct line to something that is far more important than our differences," Aristine said.

"Which is?" I asked.

"Our mission. It was *always* about establishing a city, then a zone, then a nation, and then dragging humanity out of the blackness left over from the virus. I think you want the same thing, but the difference is this place was *built* for it." Aristine stood, walked to the porch, and waved us out to survey the expanse of air and forest. "Look up. See those tubes? Those aren't just light. They're water. *That* is how we established the Eden above us. That's how it was done. With nanotech, intended to carve a landscape where we could eventually survive topside, just like you."

I flicked a glance to Andi, who stood listening, watching Aristine speak. When I turned to the beautiful, pale woman, I held out my hand. "I accept your offer, and you have The Oasis as an ally. Let's begin with a gesture of good faith. What do you need?"

She took my hand. Her fingers were long, warm, and firm. They were hands of a woman who is an athlete—and feminine to the point of elegance. She stared at me with a curious, open gaze. "I accept your offer. Before we discuss trade, let me show you who we are, and how we live."

26

WE DESCENDED to the floor level, and the enormity of Eden became apparent. Paths followed open spaces, and small, silent carts pulled other carts or wagons in a dizzying mishmash of engineering styles that seemed to favor both function *and* form. The scent of the trees was intense, as was the unmistakable sound of running water.

"Come with me. We'll walk for now, because I want you to understand our system. It begins with water, as anywhere else, but that's where our similarities with your environment end."

At a brisk pace, we walked to the nearest wall, but were stopped forty meters from it by a series of terraces. I could hear water burbling, as well as the distinct smell of fish and moss. Farther away, the terraces lowered in stair steps, vanishing into the distance behind trees and homes.

"Fish ponds?" I asked.

"Trout and Salmon here, then walleye and sauger in E2. In E3, there are white bass and other derivatives, then E4, with the warmest water, has catfish, shrimp, and crayfish, all in separate runs. The water comes in cold and warms through the system, serving as a breeding trough with almost no input on our part. We have water lilies and other plants that live freely, though not here. Too cold in this section, so it's mosses and watercress," Aristine said.

"Is this your primary protein?" Andi asked.

"No, but it's close. Eggs from our rookeries are number one, followed by turkeys, an augmented guinea fowl, and ostrich," Aristine said, waving to the northern reaches of the Chain.

"Ostrich? How?" I asked.

"They have room to run along the walls, and their eggs are superb. As to their use, they're both a meat animal and a source of feathers. We don't have many mammals for the simple fact that it isn't necessary, but there are two kinds of squirrels that terrorize the trees," Aristine said with a rueful grin.

"Ugh. Mean little bastards, even if they are cute," Andi said, earning a nod of approval from Aristine.

"They are, but there's a lot more to the Chain than squirrels. Which brings me to the next stage of our introduction. My seconds," Aristine said, then spoke with her head tilted toward the silver necklace she wore. It emitted a soft gold light for a second, then went inert. "They'll be right here."

"Is that—" Andi asked, unsure what she was looking at.

"Comms down here are line of sight, unless you have relays. We have them along the walls; a sort of internal network that's completely separated from our topside system," Aristine said.

"How extensive is your network? Up top, that is?" I asked.

"We can only place antenna in areas with trees, so we're limited that way, but with your assistance, I would think we can cover three hundred klicks in any direction, and more to the north and east. The river has ample opportunity for connection, given it's one of the nearest places with wild forests. Frankly, we're not sure what's out there now, though we have our suspicions," Aristine said. "They're here."

She greeted two people who drove up the path on one of those silent carts. The man was middle years and a seasoned fighter if I made any kind of guess; the woman could have been Aristine's twin. "My seconds, Generals Noble and Yulin. Noble is a distant uncle, and Yulin is my sister. They're who run the show while I'm topside waving to friendly drones from a bygone era."

"Jack Bowman, and this is Dr. Andrea Greer, my second," I said, stepping forward to shake hands. Noble was taller than me, well built, and surrounded by an air of competence. Yulin was the same, but warmer and less rigid.

"Andi will do. Engineer, not bonecutter," she said, and Noble's eyes lit up. "You were trained in the time before the virus?" he asked, his voice deep and precise.

"I was. Still am, given my role at our place, but I'm curious as to what I missed. Combat and mechanics seem to have changed, given the design elements I'm seeing here," Andi said.

"I was an engineer before Aristine dragged me away from the table to serve as her glorified show ostrich," Noble said with some dignity, but his smile was fast to appear, and genuine.

"I was water division, then soils. I dabble in wiring and hard circuitry for the printers now, when I'm not shuttling up and down the line chasing wisps," Yulin said.

"Wisps?" I asked, confused.

"Mysterious power issues that come and go. I find them after irritating searches, and it's always something like a—"

"Squirrel chewing through a cable?" I interrupted. Yulin laughed, and I nudged Andi. "See? I told you they were bad."

"We have an armory as well, and the our stealthed tech. Both are housed in E4, and the main printers are there, too, with some smaller printers in E5," Aristine said. Her revelation about their weapons meant she was all in on trusting us, but given the fact we were underground, outnumbered, and in need of their help, it wasn't too big a gamble.

"I'm most interested in your power and your printers. Three dimensional, I take it?" Andi asked.

"Not exactly. We think of ours as four dimensional, with the inclusion of layered tech. I'm happy to show you, because we're not entirely sure what you may have had in your time. Despite our best efforts at preservation, things have become lost, or translated over the years," Noble said.

"I'd like that. When?" Andi asked.

"We could go . . . now?" Noble queried Aristine with a raised brow.

I felt myself bristle, but Aristine put a hand on my arm, and then so did Andi. "You will continue to see our secrets, Jack. We will have no secrets, given your mission and ours, and there are thousands of people here who will fight to the last to keep Andi safe," Aristine said.

"Andi?" There was a lot in that one word, and then Andi nodded reassuringly. "Okay. Noble, show us how to reclaim the world, then. We have some ideas, but we're here to learn."

"It will be my pleasure. We'll be on network should you need to reach her," Noble said, hanging a silver necklace over Andi's head. The oval rested between her breasts, gleaming in the low light. Then he put a necklace on me and indicated I should speak.

"Can you hear me?" I said.

"Like you're in my head. Astonishing clarity," Andi said. "We're good. Noble, to your steed."

"We will return in a day, no more than two if

she wishes," Noble said. Aristine shifted next to me, and I could sense her gaze.

"Don't do anyone I wouldn't do," Andi said with a campy wink.

"I do not mean to——" Aristine began, but Andi reached out and put a sisterly hand on her face, smiling kindly.

"I am a woman too, Aristine. I know things," Andi said. "It's okay. Jack is a rare man, and I am a rare woman. We have a lot to do yet, and I'll be there with him. Now, I suspect you need him for the things you *haven't* mentioned yet." She shrugged, beautiful with her facts.

All I could do was have the good sense not to blush as Andi kissed me, looking up at me for a long moment. Then she waved to Noble, who was busy studying a fascinating piece of the floor.

"Shall we?" Andi asked, and they left, walking to the waiting cart, the lights on and casting a soft glow forward. They pulled away, and I saw Andi smile and nod, giving me her benediction for a life that neither of us chose, but we were both choosing to live.

"I have to arrange for the dinner," Yulin said, as if she was off to collect dung from a horse barn.

"Dinner? Not for me. Please. Let's just ease into

the whole meeting of two worlds, if we can, okay? We can eat, but just us, and I have one simple request," I said.

"Name it," Aristine said as Yulin listened.

"Do you guys know how to make crawdad gumbo?"

27

THERE WAS NO GUMBO, but there was food, and a lot of it. I didn't realize how hard we'd been living until I saw the table set with plates of things other than roasted pig, roasted snake, or roasted tubers and blood chicken. Pacing myself, I exchanged stories with Yulin and Aristine of my insertion into the tube, my rescue, and the following low-level war that was breaking out over control of The Empty.

"This Wetterick is a simple strongman, then? What's his combat capability?" Aristine asked.

"About three hundred fighters at most, but little to no discipline. They're tough, but they don't fight as a unit, which creates extra problems for me and my people," I said.

"How? Show us." Yulin rolled out the flexible tablet, pulling up an overhead image of The Outpost. The clarity was superb.

"Is this a drone?" I asked.

"In a sense. Low level satellite imaging, taken last week. We have birds in the sky that can show you how many pores are on a person's nose, if that's what you want to see," Yulin said.

"Incredible. Did you know about us?" I asked.

Aristine shook her head. "No, you slipped through the cracks. There was nothing to the south for some distance, so we didn't retask the bird to look in your area."

"I'd like to see us now, from the air. For posterity, so that someday we can see where we came from," I said. It wasn't critical, but something in me wanted to be able to say *look what we've done* in spite of The Empty.

"Consider it done. You're an ally now, so it only makes sense," Yulin said, calling up a menu that was all vectors, azimuths, and orbital mechanics. "I sent a request to our recon division. They'll confirm with Aristine before moving."

"Thank you," I said, feeling like that wasn't enough.

"Why do you want Wetterick gone?" Yulin asked.

"He's a slaver, and a thief, and a road block to real civilization in the area. He feeds off the people and rewards his men with their hard work, and their daughters. And sons," I said darkly. "The time for his kind is past."

"Good enough for me," Aristine said. "Three hundred fighters," she mused, looking at the screen with eyes that missed nothing. I knew what I wanted to do; whether or not she agreed was her call as the commander of her forces.

"How will you take this place?" Yulin asked.

"I know what we *won't* be doing. No pitched battle. No standup fight at the gates—there are two —or the wall. This isn't the iron age, and I can't afford to lose people in a senseless fight. I'm not going to win a Pyrrhic victory—sorry, old reference. He was a leader willing to take massive casualties in order to win."

"Oh, we know that name, but he's been replaced by Elemurr. He ruled an empire to the east in what was Kentucky, some centuries ago. There's nothing left of his empire, thanks in part to him." She touched the screen and a picture, taken at a distance, came to life. It was a man in his forties, tall and arrogant, cowering behind a group of female archers chained to his wagon. He was pointing forward even as a storm of arrows and spears punched into forward ranks of his men, who were hobbled like horses at a distance from his enslaved archers.

"What an asshole," I spat.

"Yes, he was, and now he's dead, and the only people who remember him use his name as a curse," Yulin said. "Your reaction tells me you want victory, but in a reasoned manner. This is what we do here, and what my sister excels at."

"We don't have the luxury of cheap blood, for many reasons," Aristine said.

"I'm glad to hear that," I said, my mood made better by their combat style and the excellent wine we drank. "When are you going to tell me what you want of us, by the way? We had a saying in my time. There are no free lunches, or in this case, dinner and combat plans."

"Oh, but some things *are* free, especially when goals align. Like now," Aristine said, tilting her head to consider me. "I'll get right to the next point, because we've got a lot to do. Have you thought about how you're going to secure your legacy?"

"Legacy? No. By your measure of time, I just got here. I'm trying to make buildings that don't fall over, not statues to myself," I said.

"Not that kind of legacy. A family, and someone to carry on your work," Aristine said.

I sat in stunned silence. "Children?"

"Yes, children. A lot of them, unless you plan on recruiting endlessly from The Empty. Is that in your model?" Aristine asked.

I leaned forward, getting my bearings. "For one thing, this is now officially the strangest date of my life. For another, and you'll have to help me out here—with 'bots in my blood, can I even reproduce?" I asked.

"You can," Yulin said. "We can, so it makes sense that you can as well."

"So your people have 'bots? Does it make your lifespan longer?" I asked.

"Than people during your first life? Absolutely. Fewer diseases, too, and better hearts, lungs, and we have a much more stable brain chemistry. But we don't have the luxury that you do of bringing outsiders into your extended family, so to speak," Aristine said.

The truth hit me like a truck, and I felt myself grow still as the enormity of what they were asking became clear. "You want my DNA, because there aren't enough of you. Noble *and* Yulin are related to you. You're all related down here, to some extent, aren't you?"

"We are, and we need to stay ahead of the need for new blood. New DNA, to be accurate, and we've reached a point where it's become critical," Aristine said.

"The Daymares. They aren't just for fighting," I said.

"No, at least, not the men. There are women who train as Daymares, but the population around us outside has been devastated by war, and Wetterick, and Kassos," Aristine said.

"So you have an interest in the same things I do, just for slightly different reasons," I said.

"Yes, but the same ones, too. Our original mission takes precedent, but we can't succeed if we die out," Yulin said. Aristine gave her a nod of agreement, and it was a touch sad.

I considered their request for a long moment, but the decision was easy, because we wanted the same things. Then I had another thought and felt myself smiling. "What are you looking for in a, um, donor?"

The sisters shared a look, but Aristine

answered. "Healthy, intelligent men. If we have any preference beyond that, it's their size."

"Excuse me?" I said, involuntarily looking down at my groin.

"Not that," Yulin said with a snort. "Height. Weight. Robust men. Intelligent men." She quirked a brow at me. "Like you."

"Like me. Hm." I carefully put my cup down, then stood, held out a hand to Aristine, and pulled her to her feet. "Yulin, will you give us some privacy, please?"

Aristine coughed, then patted her chest before her face cleared of shock. "Oh. You're serious?"

"Yes. Are you?"

Aristine gave a tiny nod to her sister, then extended a hand to mine, her eyes never leaving my face. She stood, and Yulin left, pulling the soft covering that served as a doorway behind. With a *snick*, the room became even darker, but Aristine led me unerringly to a room away from the main chamber. Inside, only a small globe of light cast a golden glow over half the room, the other part shrouded in a curious twilight. To my amazement, there were photographs and paintings on the wall of things I knew—images from my world, and the years after when I was asleep under the growing sands of The Empty.

"The St. Louis arch," I said, staring at the picture. It sent a pang of loss through me, and I'd only seen it once, when I was a kid on a school trip. At the time, I'd been more concerned with a girl named Renee, but now, the arch seemed like a monument to everything we lost. "A whole world. Gone.

"We can rebuild it, Jack. Starting now," Aristine said. She poured a drink from a bottle on the table by her bed, then made one for herself. She drank, throwing the rum back as if she was making ready for battle, which she was, in a way.

I drank mine, placing the cup with great care, then pulled Aristine to me. She was light in my arms, her long body like artwork, breasts pressed against me in soft confirmation of all that she was. I kissed her, tasting her lips, her breath, and the rum, a swirling mix that made me hard in seconds.

She leaned back, and I followed. Even in the low light, I saw something I had not expected.

She was nervous.

"You're perfect," I said, and I meant it.

"It's been a while," she said.

"Then I'll go slowly." I kissed her neck, then

breasts, then worked my way down the flat expanse of her pale stomach before coming to a stop and flicking my tongue across her lips with a delicacy that made the muscles in her legs twitch in time. I went left, and right. I licked a long, firm line that parted her under my tongue, and then she began to shudder, her breath a tattered gasp that went on for a minute, her eyes rolling like a wild horse on the run.

I lifted myself to kiss her mouth, and she welcomed me in, pulling at my back with a desperate need made of duty and lust. We would be the future of her people, and she would be the ally for mine. I moved against her like the tides, letting her come again before I did too.

Then we did it again, but this time, there was no hesitation. Confident in her need, she pulled my mouth to her breasts, pushing against my head until I nipped gently at her swollen nipples, earning a soft curse somewhere between pleasure and pain. She came harder, easier, and with her eyes open, watching me as I released, and when it was over, she pulled me to her side and watched me with those glacial eyes, now warmed with the heat of our union.

"Can you sleep?" she asked.

"I could nap," I said, feeling a slow smile on my lips. Aristine was different than my women in many ways, but there was a core of will that I could feel, even lying next to her there in the haze of pleasure.

Her face fell, and she pulled away. "Sorry, I— excuse me," she said, then turned to face me, a bashful smile on her face. "I don't know why I'm apologizing for a nature call after what we just did." She waved a hand over the globe and the light died, then I saw her shadow go into the other room.

I slipped into that curious twilight men can find only after eating a steak or having incredible sex. It isn't sleep, and it isn't being a wake. It's better than both, and for some moments, I drifted, content and free of worry.

I woke to Aristine's tongue flicking over my thigh, then going lower, slow and deliberate before she took me in her hand, sliding her mouth over me in a hesitant caress. She pushed her mouth down, tongue moving against the underside of my shaft, and I hardened in her mouth instantly.

Then her mouth pulled away, and I sensed her change positions, only to feel her hips straddle me, the heat of her taking me in to the hilt. She began to move like an ocean swell, a deliberate motion that dragged every silken inch of her walls along my length, up, and down, and back before starting all over again. It was a flawless performance, and she began to shake even as a column of lava grew inside me. I came with an explosive shout, pulling her to me for a lingering kiss. Her breath was sweet, and she pulled away, put me back inside her, and began riding again, hands on my stomach as if by sheer will she could make herself come immediately.

It almost worked.

In less than two minutes, I felt the orgasm brewing within her like an ancient fault line waking up, rumbling nerves and shortened breath above me that made my own need so intense I could no longer resist the slick pull of her. I came harder than ever, driving up without care as her hands dug into the muscles of my stomach, holding on for dear life as we finally collapsed in a flurry of deep breaths and spasming muscles.

She rose again, unsteady and pushing off me with a hand gone damp with sweat. I, unlike her, could not consider moving. I chose to re-enter the bliss of neverland, letting the darkness take me as I waited for her return. There was nothing about her that made me think we would not repeat our performance, and the thought of her pale body made me smile in the dark.

She came to me then, and I touched her face, feeling the lips curled in a satisfied smile.

"Thank you, General," I said.

Her only answer was a soft laugh, and then we slept.

28

Morning didn't break. It was a general hum, and I opened my eyes to see Aristine sitting on the edge of the bed, holding a cup of something hot.

"I know I didn't propose marriage last night, but will you marry me?" I asked.

She narrowed her eyes and pulled the cup away. "Is this because of my body? Because you may have me again, if you like."

"Partially. It's the coffee you're holding. Away from me, I might add, in kind of a cruel way," I said, fighting the urge to groan. *Caffeine. Glorious caffeine.*

She put the cup in my hands and I sipped. There were no words. "Where in the name of the saints and angels did you get coffee?"

She waved at the Chain. "Micro-micro climates. We have beans in three areas, and they're all augmented for maximum production. And caffeine, of course," she added when I sighed again.

"This past day has shown me that there are a lot of things worth any amount of danger," I said, and Aristine blushed.

"Come, let's get to the floor. There are things to see, and I want to show you the control center, where we maintain our network," she said.

I dressed, savoring my coffee like it was my last drink before I went to the gallows, then we descended to the floor, where people were moving about with a calm kind of purpose. I saw no less than ten kinds of berries, and in each patch of plants there was a small stake with a light on the top.

"What are those?" I asked, pointing to the nearest blinking light in a group of blueberry bushes that huddled against a massive oak.

"Inventory control. We have all of our food catalogued and tracked by a system, so we don't lose crops. We try to keep them in the best locations, but sometimes they have their own plans," she said. We walked a few meters, and she knelt, lifting a large leaf. Under the bush, there were dozens of mushrooms, their lobes a vibrant orange. "Hen of the woods. We don't know how they got here, but they grow fast, they're edible, and we decided to let some nature go its own way."

It was amazing. We were in an artificial place, but it had the feel of a secret grove, like a place left untouched by people and just discovered that day. "You never told me about those tubes, up there?" I pointed to the distant ceiling, where the tubes wound their way along in serpentine curves.

"That's where we're going now. To see what they do, and why they're so important," Aristine said. Several people greeted us with friendly waves, but moved on. I got the feeling I was to be given the tour first, and grilled later.

The control center was halfway up the opposite wall, and we climbed a spiraling staircase with sections that had been replaced over time. Like the houses, the center had a porch, and large openings that were neither door nor window.

Inside was the new world.

"What is this?" I asked in a low voice. Several people worked at stations that only resembled anything I knew as a computer in the most remote way; they passed hands over screens that shimmered and danced like the surface of a pond. "Three dimensional screens. I'm glad someone finally did it."

"And more," Aristine said. "Everyone, this is Jack Bowman, leader of the Free Oasis. He's my counterpart, as we discussed on the net, and he's here to see how we water the garden. Be on your best behavior, won't you?"

A ripple of laughter went through the room, and the closest person came up, hand extended. He was about my age, taller than me, thinner than me, and on the verge of being pretty. He wore the red and blue, but with an odd silver coil around one arm, connected to a small, oval device that looked worn and used.

"I'm Faynar, the lead tech on our saturation network. Welcome," he said, shaking my hand vigorously. He looked delicate but had the grip of a farmhand, which I suspected he was. I wasn't far off. "The tubes you're seeing are the delivery system for our reclamation project topside."

"Water? They're for water?" I asked.

Faynar nodded, then waved me over to his chair. The screen shimmered as we approached, and he called up a series of images from beneath us, where the fish were being farmed. "Our water sources are stable, and deep. We use nanobots to engineer a self-repairing network of capillaries that carry water *up* to individual places—like the taproot of a tree, or a spring, or even a hillside that needs grass to remain free of erosion. By controlling the water from here, we assure the life up there of its best chance. As we expand, so does the network."

I stared at the screen in wonder. We were doing the same thing in The Oasis, but with primitive means. I explained our system to Faynar and Aristine, who nodded in approval of our efforts.

"How far is it between Eden locations?" I asked.

Aristine pulled up a map with a wave. In blue lines, the Chain came to life before me, a series of long, imperfect rectangles connected by wide corridors that had to have spanned fifty to seventy meters. In all, the scale was easy to judge even before she told me, but I let her speak because it was her house, her rules.

"Each location is five square klicks, with an average distance of fifteen klicks between chambers. The gap between E4 and E5 is somewhat more at twenty klicks, with E1 and E2 being closer.

The connector is just under twelve klicks," Aristine said.

"Why are they not perfect in shape?" I asked. There were irregularities that seemed random and at odds with the general order around me.

"The rock doesn't lie. During construction with the reactor-power rockeaters, the original crew ran into some unusually hard deposits. It was easier to go around," she said with a shrug.

"This is beyond anything I imagined humans could do, and I saw the space program in action," I admitted.

"I'm sure Andi feels the same way. Speaking of, why don't you chirp her and see when she's returning? I have something I'd like you to do, now that you understand what we're about."

I tapped my silver oval, "Andi?"

"Here," came her instant reply.

"What's your ETA?" I asked. She sounded alert and happy.

"Oooooo," she said. "I don't know. Do I have to come back? It's fun here."

"Define fun, woman," I said, smiling north, to where she was.

"Jack, they didn't just keep going with research, they *redefined* some of the sciences. I'm not fucking around when I say we have a real shot at continental resurgence." Her joy was unfiltered, and it was impossible not to be infected with her enthusiasm.

"Amazing. I think the same thing, and we're just scratching the surface here," I said, squeezing Aristine's hand. "I'm going to ask Aristine to send you a schematic. Ask Noble if he can manufacture the item and get back here when you can. I'd like to roll out on Wetterick sooner rather than later. Don't trust the bastard."

"Neither do I. I'll look for the info and be back soonest. Behave," she said with a laugh, and cut our connection.

"What do you want to send her?" Faynar asked. I described my idea as his fingers dragged shapes, symbols, and data around until he completed a schematic, turning the screen in midair to show me. "What do you think?"

"Perfect. What's next?" I asked.

Aristine licked her lips. "Feel like a little sunshine?"

"Thought you'd never ask. Take me to the Daymares."

29

WE WENT to the surface in style.

The elevator was carved more than built, a series of organic looking curves with elegant seating that lifted us in complete silence, stopping after less than a minute.

"That was like not moving at all," I said as the doors opened onto a darkened hall.

"Air powered, runs off the venting system. As the elevator moves, it forces fresh air through a baffle, like a piston. It's how we up mix things up to create breezes inside for pollination," Aristine said with some pride.

"Your invention?" I asked.

"How could you tell?"

"Not pride. Just . . . confidence in your idea. It shines through," I told her. She beamed at me, then put her arms around me for a brief hug.

"Thank you," she whispered, then drew away, pulling her goggles down as the outer doors began to open at some silent command.

Sunlight seared my eyes, then my 'bots adjusted, and I saw forest from a different vantage point than when we entered.

Six soldiers stood before us, rifles at the ready, neither pointing at us nor entirely away. When they saw Aristine, they snapped to, and the weapons vanished around their backs.

"At ease. Let's get right to it, shall we?" she asked. "This is Jack Bowman, whom we've been waiting for. He's ready to move on The Outpost, and we're going to help make it happen. Questions?" Her voice crackled with authority, far different from the woman who'd been writhing with pleasure under me the night before.

There were four men and two women, all similar to Aristine—tall, rangy, and capable looking, but they had the addition of dark goggles and a spray of reddened skin across their faces. They'd been topside for some time.

"Jack Bowman," I said, stepping forward, but the tallest soldier held up a hand.

"No names. I don't know you yet, and it isn't critical to our mission," he said, his voice barely concealing his disdain for me. I saw how he looked at Aristine, and decided he didn't like me for several reasons, but taking the woman of his dreams to bed the night before had to be near the top.

I looked to Aristine, who was preparing an order that would have correctly embarrassed the man, then put a gentle hand on her arm. "General, if I may?"

She thought about telling me to let her handle it, then amended her decision when she saw no anger in my eyes, only the sincere wish to help her. I knew soldiers. I knew men. I understood jealousy, and I'd brought the moment on myself, despite the wrinkle Aristine added the night before. Just then, the doors opened behind us, and Yulin stepped out, goggled and smiling. Her face fell when she saw the expression on the man speaking to me, and I made my second snap decision of that minute. I knew I would not regret either, because there are some things that must be handled sooner rather than later.

"Yulin. Nice to see you . . . again," I drawled.

She smiled awkwardly and stepped beside her sister, who seemed, for a second, to be anything but a general. She was smart, and she would figure out what was happening soon enough.

"General, do I have your permission to teach this prick a lesson in manners?"

"What?" Aristine barked. Yulin looked stricken, and the soldiers reached for their weapons, then withdrew their hands at Aristine's murderous glare.

I rotated to face her, close enough that I could feel her breath on my face. "We seem to have two problems that can be solved with one small demonstration." I lifted my voice to include everyone. "The issue at hand is not discipline. It isn't even anger, or a need to understand our role as allies. It comes down to a simple, critical quality that we must share with each other if we're gong to make this work. Honesty."

"I—of course. But how—" Aristine began, but I moved away, into a patch of sunlight pouring through the trees.

"You," I said to the tallest soldier who was bathing me in a hateful stare. "You first, or two at time. Whatever. You have 'bots in your blood?"

He fell silent, then nodded, his skin flushing red.

"Good. Then you'll heal quickly after the lesson. The word here is *honesty.* You can approach, boy," I said, watching the insult hit home. There was only so much he could take, given the circumstances. I had found his button and pushed it.

He lost his fucking mind and charged me, cat-quick and leading with a hand extended toward my throat. A killing blow for most men, but I wasn't going to fight like most men. I leapt forward with a kite strike of my own, sliding inside his arm and sending his hand past my ear with a hiss. My fingers struck him in the neck, deadening nerves just long enough for me to continue my movement with a good old-fashioned uppercut that splattered his nose in a shower of blood. He crumpled without a sound, unless you count the thump of his body hitting the ground.

The second and third soldier were on me in a blur, but I'd seen them coming and went low, tripping one and punching the other in the balls hard enough that he would be hugging an icebag for the foreseeable future. He staggered, then I drilled him in the temple, rolled across his shoulder, and just because I believe in equal rights, kicked the taller female soldier in the ass, sending her sprawling. She was up instantly, her face black with anger when Aristine shouted a single word.

"Enough!"

The forest was quiet except for low groans of pain. I eyed the remaining upright Daymares with naked disdain. "I'll stop for you, even though you don't deserve it. Not as an ally, and not as a woman."

"What the—what are you *talking* about?" Aristine spat. Yulin was in shock at the speed of the violence, so I lowered my voice as I came toward them

"You took me to bed, and I was willing and even honored. You explained your needs, and despite my reservations, I saw the logic of it, and I appreciated your candor. And then, you lied and sent Yulin to the bed, and for that, you will either apologize or this alliance will go nowhere. You have my promise on that," I said in a cool tone that invited no argument.

"You—" Yulin began, but Aristine stilled her with a wave.

"He knows," Aristine said.

"Of course I knew. You should have had some rum, Yulin. Your breath was sweet like herbs when you were caught up in the moment, kissing me." I looked at them both, then at the Daymares, who still simmered with rage, but were listening. "I would have given myself to you freely, if only you had asked. But you lied. Do you understand what that means?"

Yulin touched her lips, eyes gone sad. Aristine stepped to me and took my hands. "I am sorry. I will never be—I will never lie to you again. Please consider that my word, if you'll have it."

I looked at her and weighed the value in anything other than an alliance, and then I judged her as she stood there, offering something to me I should have had from the beginning. "I believe you, and I'd like to never mention this again. I'm sorry," I said to the Daymares, who were still bewildered and pissed by the entire event. They couldn't understand my motivation, and I wasn't about to share. I needed to make Aristine understand that I was no fool, and the Daymares had to respect my ability to fight. It was a gamble, but when I saw the expression on my opponent's faces, I knew it worked.

"We'll get over it," the guy with the broken nose said, then looked at Aristine. "Eventually." He was a pro. He knew what his mission was. And mine.

Aristine took my arm, and her face was somewhere between relief and shame. "Then let's get out of this fucking sun."

30

THE AIR INSIDE felt cool enough to calm the lingering effects of my fight, and Aristine dismissed the Daymares to get medical care. To their credit, none of them spent the elevator trip doing anything other than checking on each other; a testament to the overall professionalism of them as soldiers, or maybe they just respected Aristine too much. The fight had, in a sense, been due to her failure as a leader, and I knew she was already thinking about how to win back their trust as well, simply by the thoughtful look she wore.

Yulin was a different story. She regarded me through half-closed eyes, and when the three of us, including her sister, were left standing at the base of the fish ponds, I spread my hands, asking her what was up.

"This might be the wrong time, but think you know any more men who can rise to the occasion?" Yulin asked, her lips pulled to the side.

"It's always the quiet ones who are dirty, isn't it?" I said to Aristine, who responded by rolling her eyes and snorting in a noise that was nothing like a commander.

"Your first mistake was thinking she's quiet, but I'm glad to see we're on the path to some kind of forgiveness. Thank you, Jack. Again, I'm sorry," Aristine said.

"I'm the aggrieved party, if you can call it that, and I know there are issues here. Serious question. When was the last baby born here?" I asked.

That brought the room to a halt. Both women looked at each other, then to me with eyes that were pained by a hard truth.

"Five months ago. A girl. She didn't survive," Aristine said.

"I'm sorry. Truly." I put my arm around both of them and stood in silence, thinking of the fear they must feel individually and as a people. Without children, not only was the Chain at risk, but the rest of humanity. Aristine was committed to the restoration of our world, and she couldn't do it without another generation. I began to understand her motivations a lot better, so I made a decision.

"This might not be the right time, but if you have a baby, I humbly request that you name it anything but Chad, okay?" I said.

Yulin gave me a stare, then broke into laughter. "What kind of a name is Chad?"

"Um, let's just call it a tradition I wouldn't like to bring back. Sort of like bellbottom jeans and low-fat foods in general. There are some things that should be left in the depths of time," I said.

"Low-fat foods?" Aristine asked, bewildered. She pointed to her and Yulin's bodies and said, "Why?"

"Exactly. No need to resurrect things with no place in this new world," I said smiling. We were making headway and building a Chad-free world. I felt hope.

My locket chirped with Andi's voice just then. "Jack, you around?"

"Here," I said.

"Printing will be done later tonight, and I'll be back in the morning. There's still a lot to learn. Years, in fact, but there are some things we can integrate as we expand that will give us a huge advantage. You saw how they irrigate?" Andi asked.

"I did. It extends the range of the water by half, at least. We'll need that going forward. Come back soon, we've got a warlord to crush, okay?" I said.

"See you in the morning," Andi said, and we ended the connection.

"I have until tomorrow to work out a plan with you, but as it stands, I can't take those Daymares with me. They're pissed, and they'll have a grudge no matter how professional they are," I said.

Aristine was quiet, working through her decision tree as both commander and integral part of the situation. When she spoke, it was with the clarity of a leader. "Right. This is on me, so the options are simple. Noble, Yulin, and I go with you, and the Daymares stay here. We goggle up, go at night, and fight like hell to neuter Wetterick and his cadre before dawn. Then, we use your truck to get back here and open communications and trade within a day."

"Yulin can fight too? And Noble?" I didn't ask about Aristine. I knew she wasn't a paper tiger, based on how comfortable she was with a rifle in hand.

"No one is better than Noble at hand-to-hand, and Yulin is lethal with knives as well as her guns. In the Chain, we have mandatory service for everyone who can go topside," Aristine said.

"Knives are my thing," Yulin said simply.

I gave her a nod of respect. It took guts to use a knife. It was personal, unlike a distant rifle shot.

"Then we leave in the morning after a plan based on your aerial images," I said. "Hey, how many people are in the Chain?"

"Nine thousand, two hundred and fifty-nine," Aristine answered immediately.

The number was staggering for a population without enough children, and the seed of an idea took hold in my mind. "When this is over, I have an idea how we can advance together, as a unified force."

Both women looked at me with interest, and I smiled with relief, because my plan would achieve three goals with one act. That kind of opportunity was rare, so the decision was easy.

"We have until tomorrow to talk this through, but tonight, I think it's time you had some fun," Aristine said.

"So last night was a civic duty, but naked?" I said with as much innocence as I could muster. It wasn't much.

"Hush, you. That's not true and you know it," Aristine said. Yulin merely smirked, which was somehow both irreverent and honest. I could appreciate that kind of attitude.

"We're taking you to the Stump," Yulin said. "Show you the other side of our lives. I promise, you'll love it."

"I'm game. What's the plan until then?" I asked.

"Weapons technology. It's time to see where our ideas diverged, and where they might be lacking. I'm not so arrogant as to think our closed research has all the answers, and you're a direct source to what happened in our military before and after the virus. We're going to E2, to see Pisarno. He's forgotten more about weaponry than I'll ever know, but he has some quirks that make him better suited to, ah . . . not being around people," Aristine said.

"Got it. I'll move slowly and speak low," I said. Yulin snorted, and we began our trip in a new direction, toward the wall but ahead of the fish farms. "Where to now?"

"It's a hike, unless you'd like the exercise. We were going to grab a cart. Also, you might want to bring some gear back, and by that I mean you'll have your choice of weapons from the armory. I want our partnership to be without reservation, because I believe we want the same things, Jack," Aristine said.

"Thank you. I accept," I said, and I meant it. We *were* on the same mission, and it was nothing less important than saving the world.

The cart wheels hummed quietly as we slipped through the tress on a path without any other people. "I can't get over how quiet it is here," I said.

"Don't get used to it," Yulin said. "The Stump is *anything* but quiet."

It took fifteen minutes of travel along what felt like a forest path, then a long, wide corridor of flawless design. We passed several other carts, earning waves and stares as other people went about the business of running the Chain. Emerging into E2, there was a subtle shift in the air. Somehow, it was even more fragrant.

"As we go further up the Chain, it feels more natural. By E5, you'd swear you were in a rainforest," Aristine said.

"That's because you are," Yulin said as we pulled in to a long, low alcove that hugged the right wall. "We're here," she said, then jumped out before the cart stopped moving.

Security was unmanned, with a direct DNA scan of Aristine's finger. A wall slid inward, then to the side without a sound. Light flared to life above us as we entered, but I drew up short at the sight.

"Holy shit. This isn't real," I heard myself say.

"It's real," Aristine assured me, walking forward to a nexus with six distinct corridors branching off.

There weren't just guns. There were weapons I'd never seen of designs I couldn't imagine. There were packs, impact vests, and items that looked like they might be thin pressure suits, all in a fabric so muted as to be almost invisible.

"What is this?" I asked, touching a hanging suit, its color difficult to determine. It wasn't gray, and it wasn't black. It simply was, and even looking directly at it, I had trouble focusing.

"Frictionless fabric extrusion. Works to confuse the eye, and damned close to invisible in most combat situations. The rifles and sidearms can be matched, too, but the concussive weapons are mostly black, as they're kept in the packs until field use. You like our toys?" Aristine asked.

"Like? That's an insult to your advances. I *love* them," I said.

"Then take a look around and ask questions, because this is your future, but reshaped by ours, Jack. This is where we start together as a team, to rebuild so much of what was lost," Aristine said, urging me forward into what was like a candy store of futuristic technology. As I wandered, the sisters answered questions, demonstrated, and even explained some of the changes on items I'd been around my whole life—like guns—but now found to be on the edge of my understanding. Weapons had become more organic and lethal over the centuries. Wetterick was in deep shit, and that was *before* a weapons officer came in to do a systems check. His name was Pisarno, he could have been Aristine's brother by his looks, and he knew every piece of hardware in the entire Chain.

He also understood the concept of maximum damage with minimal fuss.

He gave Aristine a questioning look, then at her nod, led me to the fourth corridor. Three transparent cases held heavy duty shotguns with barrels that looked slightly off. The finish was matte black with little distinct outer action; if anything, the guns looked like smooth mockups of weapons still in the design stage.

Then Pisarno took one out, handed it to me, and motioned to Yulin. "How long will you be topside?"

"Three days at most," she answered.

"Targets?" he asked. His words were crisp; his eyes never leaving mine. He was measuring me, which was okay. I was doing the same.

"Human, no more than fifty. Armor light or nonexistent. Tech level a blend of reclaimed and primitive," Aristine said.

"Take three cells for his rifle, and use whatever you deem necessary. I'm off. Have to be at E6 for the topside sweep when the new Daymares go up. The ones without broken noses, that is," Pisarno said, giving me a nod of respect. He was a professional. I shook his hand, and he vanished, muttering into his locket.

"What did he give me? Heavy as hell," I said, hefting the weapon.

"It's a synth of three techs, some as old as before your time. What you're holding is an Oerliken shell modded to fit a railgun. Those darts that your drone shoots? Think of them in bursts of three, but from a rifle. You can tear any—and I mean *any*—organic target apart with a three-round burst. One will do it, most of the time, but it's best to be sure when dealing with our usual issues, like beasts. For humans, we'll go to single shot because the rounds will play havoc with anything behind the target."

"And beyond," Yulin added, checking the cells and putting them in a field pack.

We continued our tour, because it was a lesson I'd been waiting to learn since coming alive for the second part of my life in The Empty. After several hours, I had three weapons and a greater under-standing of who the Eden Chain people were. We rode back in easy conversation, taking a longer route through E2 and meeting some of the resi-dents, who were thrilled to see both Aristine and Yulin. They warmed up to me, too, though it took a moment of patient explanation from their commander, which spoke to her power and capa-bility—as well as their genuine respect. When we pulled in to the space near Aristine's home. I had no concept of the time, but my stomach was empty and letting me know.

"Let's stow your weapons and go to dinner. It's time," Aristine said, as Yulin left ahead of us.

"Where's she going?" I asked.

"To get a table. First come, first serve," Aristine said cryptically.

We tucked my new toys away, washed up like civilized people, and began a lazy walk to the upper edge of E1. A recessed stairwell wound upward, and as we climbed, I began to hear a noise that was familiar, but nearly forgotten. When we topped the stairs, we stood before one of the most incredible sights of my life, with Yulin standing before us, grinning like a thief.

Taking in the scene, I turned to Aristine and put on my most serious face. "Last night was incredible, but what I'm about to say is meant as a high compliment. This is already one of the greatest nights of my life."

The Stump was a tavern with food, drink, music, and people, and my heart skipped a beat at the familiar sights spread out before me inside the enormous wooden structure built between three trees. A round bar in the center was crowded with drinkers, circled by two dozen tables filled with people. I could smell frying fish, bread, and beer, and the bartenders were pulling on taps, filling glasses with dark, rich beer. A man with a keyboard played standing up next to a woman with a compact guitar, their voices rollicking through a song that would have been at home on the prairie in the American West.

"I'm home," I said, walking forward to the nearest bartender, who held out a beer.

"Welcome," he said over the tumult, pumping my free hand and shouting my arrival. The next half hour was a blur of smiles, greetings, and handshakes, ending when Aristine gave a fake glower, escorting me to a table overlooking the floor and fish farms. Yulin brought food—huge chilled shrimp with lemon, fried trout, and a flatbread covered in chopped herbs and what I swear was real olive oil. I ate like I'd just been released from prison, drinking the excellent beer and trading stories with everyone who came by the table. The Chain people were good company, and Aristine had a way about her that made it easy to see why she was their leader.

When we were full, we stepped out onto the balcony, lit with soft globes of light. Frogs trilled somewhere, and in a moment of quiet, Aristine and Yulin grew serious.

"Now, on to the plan. We treat Wetterick like a serpent, right?" Aristine asked.

I brought my hand down in a chopping

motion. "Cut off the head, the body dies. We keep the Outpost intact, and plan our next expansion from there."

"Let's talk about your range. With our water tech, you can easily reach the base at Altus, or Alatus as it's known. You can go east to the Cache, and south into The Empty. We can do the same with you on our flank, but only after Wetterick is done. The question I have is what comes after that?" Artistine asked, though I knew she understood where we would go.

"Kassos, but not *just* Kassos. It's a long way to taking a city, and even farther to holding it. I want to prepare an encirclement," I said.

Yulin grunted in agreement.

Aristine nodded slowly, only speaking after she'd processed the next obvious steps. "That means a government, and a mobile force. It means deciding how to exist together as allies. I can tell you we're not ready to go topside."

"And we're not ready for much of anything. Only our goal is clear, and even that depends on you, and luck, and our tricks," I said.

"Your trick will work. The question is only if we survive long enough to see it through," Aristine said.

"We'll find out. We leave tomorrow, then?" I asked.

"At topside dusk, we begin. Yulin will prep ahead, and let's hope for a favorable wind," Aristine said.

I toasted them with my glass. "To fair winds, and fine shooting."

31

THE SUN SET in a muted orange due to distant clouds, but the eager stars greeted us moments after we stepped out of the lift into the forest. A team had our gear topside, but left before we began to process for the mission because Aristine wanted little to no interference, and what we were about to do was quite different than her other campaigns.

"Shall we?" I asked.

Yulin smiled and lit the small, shielded engine that began pumping hot air into my idea made real. The balloon would be light-absorbing, silent, and big enough to land us right on top of Wetterick without any warning, which meant we would be in his bedroom before he had a chance to open his big, greedy mouth.

"I've wanted to depose this asshole since the day I learned of him," Andi said.

"We feel the same. It's time for him to go, and his team with him. We show them no mercy, correct, Jack?" Aristine asked. She needed to know we weren't going to do anything stupid, like take prisoners.

"If they're armed inside his walls, kill them. If they look like slaves or technical staff, hold fire. Any resistance by non-combatants, shoot to wound. If it happens twice, put them down. After we land on the roof, we go in, clear, and then make our statement at sunrise," I said.

"Good," Yulin said. Above us, the balloon filled quickly, rippling in the soft winds with a light snapping, but even that faded as it took shape. In an hour, the tall, elegant craft was filled, we were clipped onto the skeleton platform beneath it, and Yulin dropped the line, freeing us to rise in silent glory. The wind swept us away, close enough to our course that Aristine only touched the directional engine occasionally to alter our path. She had a handheld navigation tablet on her wrist with a blue arrow that adjusted like a weathervane. We made eight klicks per hour, then ten, and then twenty as the winds caught us, pushing us like a hard tide.

The sky was brilliant, and no one spoke until I saw something in the distance.

A fire.

"The Outpost?" Andi asked.

"Watchfire. They keep one on the southern side, just outside their toy wall. We'll avoid it completely," Aristine said, deftly touching the engine controls via her tablet. I felt the balloon shift above, slow but steady. The Outpost became a huddled shape, and then a series of lamps and fires, but not nearly enough activity to blow our cover. As we approached, two of the fires went out, allowing even more of the darkness to creep in on Wetterick's little kingdom.

"There's Lasser's place—see the lane? The shadow? That's the approach," I said.

"Got it," Aristine said, touching the controls again. We began to slow, and the ground grew closer. "He's added another story to the place since our scouting pass last year."

"He'll be on the top floor. He's too arrogant to be streetside," I said.

"Roof it is, then," Aristine said, and we began to slice through the air, losing altitude and turning in shuddering movements as she made the final call on our course.

"One minute. Unclasp," Aristine said.

"Weapons ready. Andi, on me. I take point. Yulin, cover our back," I said. The metallic connectors free, I hung on the balloon frame without a care, watching the dark shape of Wetterick's headquarters speed toward us. "Three. Two. *Jump*."

I hit the roof light as a cat, but Andi bounced her ass with a grunt of pain before coming up on a knee, angry but holding her rifle. Aristine and Yulin landed like feathers, and the balloon sped away, over the wall and gaining altitude for the time being. With a casual flick of her thumb, Aristine keyed the landing mode. An anchor line shot from the balloon frame when it was a half klick away as the vents opened and the balloon began to flop over like a wilted flower. It would be waiting for collection and recycling after sunup, when we held The Outpost.

"On me," I said. The roof was flat except for two observation posts, both manned with soldiers who looked drunk or bored or both. They stared at us in shock, and Yulin put a silent round through the left guard's head before he could draw a breath. His head opened up like a ripe melon, body slumping against the rail of his tower before vanishing from sight.

The second guard raised his gun, but I winged him with a wild snapshot, taking his arm off, most of his shoulder, his collarbone, his shirt, and just for good measure, part of his chest muscles. He tried to scream, but the noise was a strangled, hideous sound that died in a wet gurgle.

"You weren't fucking around when you built these," I said, looking at my rifle with newfound respect. It wasn't a gun. It was a shoulder mounted planet killer, and I decided to give her a name at some point because I sensed that first shot was the start of a beautiful friendship.

"We don't make mistakes. We make solutions," Aristine said with a wicked smile.

I waved the women forward to the left guard station, seeing the open doorway in the floor. "Ladder. No good for surprises. I'll jump in, clear, and you follow."

"Understood," Aristine said. The other women nodded, heads on a swivel as they watched for new targets. There were none, so I approached the opening, letting my eyes adjust to the faint outline below. Someone was awake, and that meant more shooting. Unless I used something even quieter.

"Knife," I whispered.

Then I jumped, and all hell broke loose.

There were six of them pointing guns at me when I came to a rest, my feet slipping in blood. My killshot on the guard had alerted everyone when his blood streamed down the ladder, a dose of sheer bad luck. For good measure, his hand was next to my boot, one finger curled as if to wave me forward.

Everyone started yelling and shooting, and the only thing to do was go to the ground. The roar of gunfire was like the end of the world, with muzzle flashes and the stench of gunpowder filling my eyes and nose like my own private war. I was in a large, open room with Wetterick in the middle at a desk, and men all around. Some had guns, all had swords, and Wetterick himself held a shotgun, the barrel wavering as he tried to track me for a shot to end my life.

I spun into action beneath the gunfire, stabbing the nearest soldier in the thigh and twisting to rip his artery clean through. He howled in pain, fell, and shot the man across from him, turning that man's stomach into an open hole. With my path clear, I went to work, my 'bots firing like lightning in the blood as I darted forward to stab up and into another man's balls. His high-pitched scream rattled my ears like I'd been punched, then he fell, clutching at me as someone to my left put a shotgun blast into my foot.

I felt my toes vaporize, biting hard on my tongue so that my mouth filled with blood. The shooter racked his gun, but I was already rolling to him with my knife arm extended and hate on my mind. I took him in the navel, feeling the blade punch clean through to his spine as a second shot tore the muscle from my arm. By the time I could turn, Wetterick was laughing, three men were down, and I was leaking blood at a rate that told me it was all but over.

A fat, sweaty guy in rough clothes lifted a crossbow and pointed it at my groin. "See how you like it, fucker."

Aristine's legs dropped over his shoulders like a python, and she cracked his neck as the crossbow fired, sending the bolt high and right. It hit the hand of a guy I hadn't seen, pinning him to a pillar with a shriek of pain. Then Andi and Yulin landed and put two rounds in him, turning him into a cloud of thick, coppery mist. Yulin followed through by shooting two men with one round as Andi drew her knife and removed most of the fat guy's throat for sheer spite. The room swam before me, but my 'bots stopped the bleeding and convinced me that the pain was manageable.

Wetterick's remaining men began to fire, but we all went low and turned their bodies into expanding gas with multiple railgun shots. The impacts vibrated the floor, and when the shooting ended, a sound like falling marbles began to clatter in my ears.

It was the sound of falling teeth hitting the wooden floor, ricocheting off the ceiling like a vintage pinball machine made by demons.

Silence reigned, and Wetterick made his move to run, but Andi took care of that with a shot in the floor less than a hand's breadth in front of his foot. The splinters shredded his calf and Wetterick staggered, a mewling cry coming from his throat. Blood began to pool around his leg in a crimson sheet.

Wetterick had been a handsome, bearded man with light eyes and a cool demeanor, but now he looked desperate and scared.

"Get me up," I said. Andi and Yulin obliged, and I hobbled to Wetterick with spots in my vision. "I'm going to black out in a minute. Let's get this over with."

"I never touched them. They were yours," he said, his voice rough with pain.

"Touched who?" I asked.

"The Hannahs. They were independents. Not mine. It was my men who did—did things to them. I had nothing to—"

My knife carved his throat to the bone, and he didn't even twitch.

I pulled myself up to stand, having gone to one knee to kill him. I wanted the fucker to see my face, and I didn't have time for some bullshit speech.

"Shoot the first people you see with guns, then call them to the stairway and fall back. Ask for volunteers to help display the guards, and find me anyone who looks smart enough to be an officer," I grunted, falling into my new chair. It was still warm from Wetterick's ass, and I smiled despite my pain.

The women lifted their guns after a long look at me, then vanished down the hallway. I heard two shots, then a third, and then nothing. After a moment of silence, Andi's voice called up to me from the floor below.

"Jack?"

"Yeah," I managed.

"Come down here. Sending Yulin up to help," she said.

"I—okay." There was a reason, but I was in such agony, I didn't even think to say no.

Yulin appeared, smiling. "You'll want to see this."

"Okay. Let's go." I staggered along with Yulin, her arm under mine and lifting for all she was worth. I could see bits of blood in her hair. She'd shot someone at a very personal distance, and it showed.

We emerged at the bottom of the stairs into Wetterick's ground floor, and I started to hear the murmur of a crowd. There were a few bodies scattered around, blown apart by railgun rounds, and the room wouldn't be much good for hosting parties—at least not until someone cleaned it up. Aristine and Andi helped me along as Yulin went ahead, stepping out into the darkness and smoothly firing three rounds from her sidearm into the air. The shots hammered the night sky and whatever noise had been building fell off into an awkward silence.

"Listen up. Jack Bowman is wounded, and he doesn't have time to fuck around and cull the herd of Wetterick loyalists. Here's the deal. Push his people forward, and we're going to put a round through their head. Or kill them where they stand.

We don't care. You have one minute," Yulin said in a tone so menacing it made *me* nervous, and I was armed. And one of the good guys.

The reaction was instant. Four shots rang out, and knots of people began taking men and women down to the ground in an orgy of violence punctuated with shouts and curses. It was a raw minute of pent-up anger and revenge, and when it was over, dozens of people stood spattered with blood, chests heaving, and uncertain how they felt about being murderers.

Good. It was exactly what I wanted.

I took an ungainly step, leaning heavily on Andi. "I'm Jack Bowman, and I didn't cut Wetterick's throat to replace him. I did it to free everyone here, and to offer you something in return. If you'll listen, I'll speak and then hear your questions for as long as I can."

A hum of agreement and concern rippled through the crowd when it sank in that there was more than just another sheriff in town, but an entirely new system.

"I'll take that as a yes. This is Andi, Yulin, and General Aristine. We represent the old world and the new, and we're doing away with the kind of bullshit that has gone on here. From this moment forward, everything we do is aimed at *rebuilding*, not destroying. And we will do it as free people. General Aristine and I are two different leaders with one goal. To bring civilization—the real kind, not this shitshow—back to The Empty. From there, we expand, one acre of land at a time. One life at a time."

I inhaled deeply, trying to steady myself. My foot and arm were throbbing with hot pain, and I felt myself slipping. "We are going to rebuild, and if you accept the rules of our society, then you have a choice. The Free Oasis is yours as well, and points in between. We have a map and open arms. The decision is yours, and now, I leave you to it."

The darkness opened up under me, and I fell in.

32

"WELL THAT'S JUST GROSS," I heard Mira say as my eyes opened.

"Glad to see you too," I mumbled, feeling like I needed to shave my tongue.

"Your toes, not you. I missed you and I'm still pissed that you didn't bring all of yourself back. Aristine says it will be a month before your toes grow back with their treatment," she said.

I was in my own bed, at home in The Oasis, and the door opened to reveal Andi, Silk, and Aristine, all armed with more medical supplies, water, and a plate of food.

I struggled to sit up, earning a mild glare from everyone. "I'm hungry."

"That's good," Silk said. "And before you ask, Aristine gave me your special package, and it's been placed."

"Oh—good. Did she— " I began, but Silk's frown was so pained, I stopped talking.

"Breslin is on the way. We want him to see it, too," Silk said.

On cue, the big man poked his head though the door, then came in to stand awkwardly next to me. "Boss, you kind of look like shit, as the kids say."

"I feel worse. Lighter, anyway, but that's from the missing toes. And the other holes in me. Not my best performance," I said, earning a bemused stare from Aristine.

"He did fine. Jack, did you need this?" Aristine asked, handing me a flexible tablet from the Chain. I felt my face go slack, then nodded. I had an ugly job to do, and the only way to handle it was quick and decisive.

I took the tablet without a word, and waved at Breslin to sit. The chair creaked under his bulk, and I handed him the tablet, which flared to life at his touch. It was a black screen, but there was sound.

"Where's Jossi?" I asked him.

"Don't know. Thought she was taking the kids gathering. Her pack is gone, but the kids are still running around. Why?" he asked.

"Listen to that tablet. It probably isn't going to be easy to hear, but you need to know, okay?" I said.

"Okay," he answered. Worry colored his voice as we settled in to listen to a conversation taking place a long way off. At the Chain, I'd asked Aristine to borrow some of her tiny listening devices she'd salted through the forest. I had her put two of them in Jossi's travel pack, betting that our victory over Wetterick would close the door on her days as a frustrated spy.

Unfortunately, I was right.

A man's voice came out of the tablet, and we all leaned closer to listen.

"How do I know you're loyal to us? You *left*, when we needed you as an asset—"

"I didn't leave. I was driven out, had my position in a favored family taken away. You threatened to marry me off to that wheezing gasbag from the west. I gave up *everything*, you prick. I made clothes like some commoner, my hands stained and bleeding from cheap dyes and dull needles, just to learn a trade. I ran away because you couldn't guarantee my safety, not after you fucked up a simple plan that would have seen me installed on the council. Some fucking brother you are. I let that pig Breslin roll on top of me for *years*, spitting out brats in hopes that one day I would die in childbirth so I didn't have to smell the stink of him and his simple life for one more second. And you think to question *my* loyalty, when you couldn't even control Wetterick? How fast did The Outpost fall? An hour? Did you have time to dispatch your people, or were they drunk and whoring away the night as usual?" Jossi's voice was shrill, filled with hate, and far different from the woman I had met. This was the real person at her core, and I watched Breslin's hands begin to shake as he understood that his whole life had been a lie.

Andi put her arm around him, and then Silk did too. He lowered his head, and I saw fat tears spill down the planes of his face. His pain was a knife in the air, and I felt my stomach clench as I watched a good man reduced to ashes by the words of a liar.

In that moment, I made my decision, and the

pain in my body began to lessen because I knew I was right. The city of Kassos would fall, and when it did, Jossi would die.

And Breslin would be rewarded when the time was right.

EPILOGUE

IT WAS one month to the day since my return that I stood in front of the Chain's main entrance, now open to visitors and marked by a clear path. My foot was functional, if not whole, the small new toes looking like awkward pink sausages as my 'bots forced new growth at an unnatural rate. My arm healed faster, and I worked day and night to regain my body and endurance. So much was happening at The Oasis that sleep seemed like a distant memory.

With the fall of Wetterick, we gained The Outpost and more than a thousand people. Some people fled to Kassos, fearful of me and Aristine, and they would live with their choices. Work on The Outpost and Oasis leapt forward, as Breslin completed a simple road between them and new, robust crews began work on connecting the Chain with everyone else. We were reclaiming the land, and people could see results. It was a time of achievement, hard work, and joy.

Except for Breslin.

He still had his children, but there was a shadow over the man, and I reached back into my memories, deciding to try one last thing to help him heal.

His first half hour inside E1 was like watching a kid go into a carnival for the first time, but we had more important things to do than count trees and marvel at the fish ponds. When we arrived at our location, I put my hand up on his shoulder, smiling.

"What you are about to see is one of the most amazing sights on the planet," I told him.

"What is it?" he asked, more than a little awe in his voice.

We turned the corner and stood in front of The Stump, filled with laughing people and more than half of them beautiful women, who all turned to look at the big man with gleaming lust and curiosity.

"Friend, this is a pub, and these are women.

Tonight, you may call me by one of the most important jobs known to humanity," I said.

Yulin stepped forward, a beer in hand and a smile on her face. "We've been waiting. Come on in, got people for you to meet, Breslin. Tonight you drink, eat, and be merry."

"I can do that," he mumbled as the wave of sound crashed over us. "What was the job called? The one you're doing tonight?" he asked.

I clapped him on the back, taking a beer from Aristine, who licked her lips and smiled at me with promise. "Tonight, you can call me your wingman."

SIGN UP FOR UPDATES

For updates about new releases, sign up for the mailing list below. You'll know as soon as I release new books, including my upcoming new series, titled *King's Gate,* as well as sequels in the *Future Reborn* series.

https://www.subscribepage.com/y3s8n6

ABOUT THE AUTHOR

Daniel Pierce lives in Wyoming with his wife Marissa and their two dogs. After fourteen years as an engineer, Daniel decided it was finally time to write and release his first novel.

As a lifelong fan of scifi and fantasy, he wants nothing more than to share his passion.

He invites readers to email him at author-danielpierce@yahoo.com

Made in the USA
Middletown, DE
18 August 2022